DECATUR DEAD

Book Two in the SKYE SOUTHERLAND Cozy Mystery Series

DEBORAH MALONE

A LAMP POST BOOK

DECATUR DEAD
By Deborah Malone

ISBN 13: 978-1-60039-236-8
ebook ISBN: 978-1-60039-742-4

www.lamppostpubs.com

DECATUR DEAD

Book Two in the SKYE SOUTHERLAND Cozy Mystery Series

BY DEBORAH MALONE

He had no beauty or majesty to attract us to him,
nothing in his appearance that we should desire him.

Isaiah 53:2 (NIV)

DEDICATION

I'd like to dedicate *Decatur Dead* to editor extraordinaire, Beverly Nault. She has been right there with me and my characters through all six books and her ability to polish the gemstone never ceases to amaze me. Thank you Beverly for all your help. I look forward to working with you in the future.

I would, also, like this dedication to go to my cousin Donna Thompson. Donna has tirelessly taken care of her husband Matt, who has Alzheimers, for many years. She has done so lovingly and with selfless care. Donna, I love you and you are an inspiration to me. Let's keep up those Skype sessions.

Last but not least, for all the caregivers around the world who day after day quietly take care of their loved ones and never get the recognition they so deserve.

Alzheimers:
According to the Alzheimer's Foundation at www.alz.org

The number of Americans living with Alzheimer's disease is growing — and growing fast. An estimated 5.4 million Americans of all ages have Alzheimer's disease in 2016.

- Of the 5.4 million Americans with Alzheimer's, an estimated 5.2 million people are age 65 and older, and approximately 200,000 individuals are under age 65 (younger-onset Alzheimer's).

- One in nine people age 65 and older has Alzheimer's disease.

- By mid-century, someone in the United States will develop the disease every 33 seconds.

These numbers will escalate rapidly in coming years, as the baby boom generation has begun to reach age 65 and beyond, the age range of greatest risk of Alzheimer's. By 2050, the number of people age 65 and older with Alzheimer's disease may nearly triple, from 5.2 million to a projected 13.8 million, barring the development of medical breakthroughs to prevent or cure the disease. Previous estimates based on high range projections of population growth provided by the U.S. Census suggest that this number may be as high as 16 million.

The race is on to find a cure for this devastating disease. I mentioned in *Decatur Dead* that organophosphates was used in the treatment of Alzheimer's disease. This is true. In 1986, testing began for tacrine, the first cholinesterase inhibitor to be tried for Alzheimer disease; it was released for clinical use in 1993. Although, this particular drug is no longer in use, research continues using organophosphates. My heart goes out to all the families dealing with this debilitating and life-changing disease.

DECATUR
DEAD

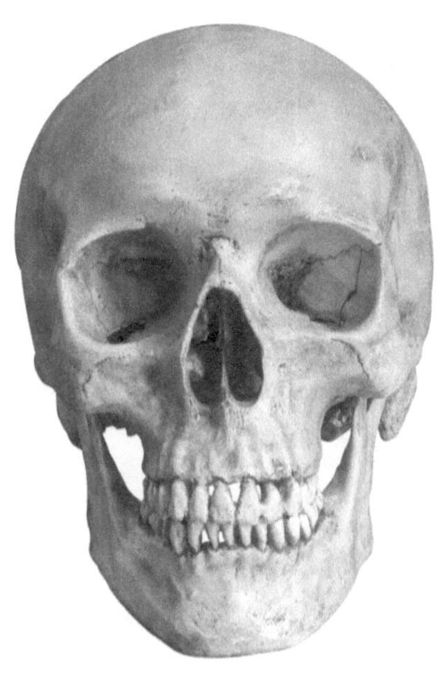

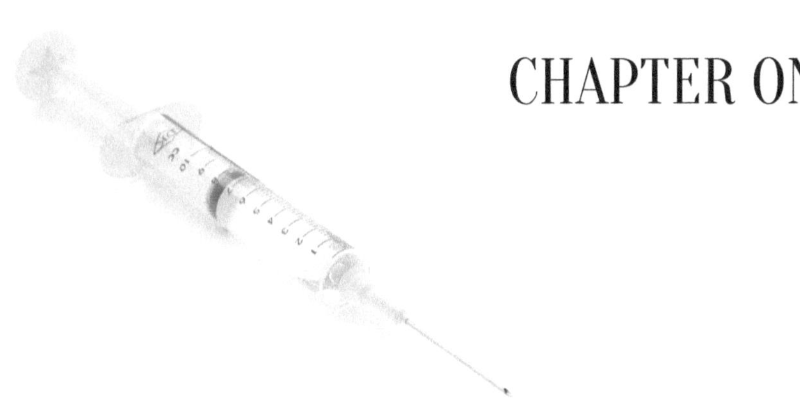

CHAPTER ONE

"What are *you* doing here?" Joan demanded, glaring at my friend Ginger.

Honey stepped from my side to wedge herself in between the two women, and Joan transferred her gaze to look into Honey's piercing stare. She leaned back ever so slightly. Even though Honey reached all of five-foot-two, her presence made her seem much taller.

"What's your problem, Joan?" Honey barked.

Joan sputtered her next words. "I want to know what that hussy," she flicked a manicured claw at Ginger, "is doing at the country club."

Ginger pushed Honey aside. "Who are you calling a hussy?"

"You. I know who you are. Just because you've weaseled your way into the club doesn't change the fact that you're a husband stealer. I know you had an affair with my husband."

"And just who is your husband?" Ginger stood her ground.

"Dr. Daniel Smith," Joan said.

Ginger's mouth flew open as she drew in a quick breath. "He told me he wasn't married. Anyway, that was in my former life. I'm a new person now."

The part about Ginger being a former exotic dancer was true. The other parts I wasn't so sure about.

Honey turned to me. "Skye, say something."

"Let's take this outside." I tried to herd them toward the exit, but either Joan didn't notice the on-lookers or she didn't care.

"Well, I'd always heard you can't teach an old dog new tricks. You are not welcome in this club and it'll be over my dead body before you become a member."

One of the bad habits we had been working on recurred as Ginger's tongue jumped the gun before she put her mind in gear. "Don't be surprised if you wake up dead one day." A collective gasp reverberated throughout the lobby and it became so quiet you could have heard a tennis ball drop.

I wished the floor would open wide and swallow me whole. I never have enjoyed being the center of attention. Unfortunately, I'd learned the hard way, having Honey and Ginger in tow were synonymous with attracting attention. Ginger's comment had left Joan speechless for a New York minute before she found her voice.

"You've been warned." Joan turned on her heels, dismissing us, leaving behind a disaster in her wake. The bewildered crowd dispersed and went on their way now the show had ended, but they cast a few pointed glances back at us.

"What in the world just happened?" I glanced over my shoulder at Joan stomping toward the door.

"Joan's always been bossy, but that was downright mean. I feel sorry for her though, everybody knows her husband's a philanderer." Honey laid her hand on Ginger's arm. "You all right, sugar?"

Ginger took a minute to speak. "Gosh, I feel terrible. I remember her husband and I swear, he really told me he wasn't married. I'm beginning to see how my old life not only affected me, but others as well."

I'm Skye Southerland, interior designer. Honey Truelove's been my right hand for the past ten years. Several months ago, her cousin Ginger showed up and asked for help in turning her life around. Honey roped me into helping, and after some initial doubts, I'd grown quite fond of Ginger.

Honey grabbed Ginger's arm. "Come on, Joan's ruined this place for me today. We can come back another time."

"She's not going to be too happy when she finds out I'm already a member," Ginger snorted.

My phone played my newest ringtone, and I looked to see the caller's identity. It was my husband and staunch supporter. "Hi, Mitch!"

"Hi babe!" Even though we'd been married more years than I cared to remember, I still experienced a little thrill at the sound of his voice. "I called to see what you're doing."

"Well, you're not going to believe this, but Joan Smith just confronted Ginger. She was furious that she'd come to the club with us." I motioned for Honey and Ginger to go ahead and I'd catch up with them.

"Why would she care if Ginger came to the club?"

I stepped into the bathroom for a little privacy. I checked under the stall doors to make sure they were unoccupied and sat on a closed commode to rest my dogs for a minute. "It's a long story and I'll fill you in later, but it seems that Ginger had an affair with her husband, not knowing he was married. Joan hasn't forgotten and took it out on Ginger. You should have seen the crowd her escapade drew."

"Skye, I hear an echo. Are you in the bathroom?"

I felt my face turning red. "Yes. I didn't want anyone to hear me so I ducked in here."

His deep, rich laughter flowed through the phone. "I called to let you know I'd be late for supper, so don't wait for me. I have a delivery of new furniture and want to get it cataloged before I come home."

"I'm with the girls, so maybe we can get a bite while we're out." The stall door opened and a rotund woman, dressed in a too-tight tennis skirt, gave me the once over. I pulled the door closed again with my free hand. "I guess I'd better go now," I lowered my voice, "I love you, and I'll see you when you get home."

"I know this is probably a moot point, but please be careful. Especially with those two in tow." His chuckle lightened my mood. After our goodbyes, I tucked my phone back in my cluttered purse and caught up with Honey and Ginger at the car.

"What happened? I was about to call Robert," Honey said. Robert

Montaine's her boyfriend. A police detective we'd met when he worked a homicide case in which Honey and I were suspects. They weren't exclusive yet, but I could see it coming.

"You just want an excuse to call Robert. I know you too well." Ginger emitted a smoker's laugh made gravelly and deep from years of rough living.

Honey placed her hands on her hips. "You might be right." Her mouth turned up at the corners. "Come on, let's blow this joint." She grabbed Ginger by the arm and led her toward my Toyota Highlander. Honey owned a sporty red Chrysler Crossfire, but when we rode together we took my vehicle. My Highlander's day job consisted of carrying supplies and swatches for my business. It hauled us around without complaint.

Honey and Ginger took turns riding in the front. Honey called shotgun. "Who was that on the phone? You were awful secretive." She pulled down the mirror and applied her signature Merle Norman Romance Red lipstick she wore year round. She smacked her lips. "Ooo – lookin' good."

"It was Mitch. I was trying to find some privacy."

"So you could talk all lovie-dovie?" Honey punched my arm. Ginger giggled. I was glad they enjoyed a good time at my expense. "You going to wear that teddy I bought you tonight? I told you it'd liven up your marriage." Another wave of laughter overtook the girls.

A few months ago Honey dragged me into Victoria's Secret for some impromptu shopping. She tried to talk me into getting a pink teddy, and when I balked she bought it for me. She said it would "crank Mitch's tractor." I had to admit it spiced up our love life, but I had no intention of sharing that information. Ever since Ginger was added to the mix, the balance of modesty had been off kilter. But I had to admit it was kinda fun to experience the feeling of a young woman in love again.

"Look you two, Mitch will be late getting home tonight. How about we get something to eat?"

"Good idea. I'm in the mood for some good ole' down home cooking. Let's hit the OK Café." Honey claimed this to be her favorite restaurant.

The café was on West Paces Ferry Road – the same road where the governor's mansion was located. We arrived early, beating the evening crowd.

Decked out in a white and black uniform fashioned from the fifties, Andi our waitress, took our beverage order. We studied the menus while we waited for our drinks.

"Can you believe Joan? She had the nerve confronting Ginger right in front of a crowd at the club. Everybody knows her husband has a roving eye."

I nudged Honey with my foot. "Shh, here comes the waitress."

She plopped down our teas, grabbed the pencil stuck behind her ear, licked the end and poised it over a greasy tablet. "Okay, I'm ready." We kept it simple and ordered vegetable plates all around. When she was out of earshot we continued our conversation.

"I don't know why she picked on me. I can't be the only one he told he was single." Ginger took a swig from her sweet tea and wiped her mouth. "Yum, good."

"Well, I feel sorry for her. Can you imagine how terrible she feels knowing the whole town gossips about her husband?"

"You're right, Skye. I'll try to be more understanding and give her a little slack. Maybe if we're lucky we won't see her anytime soon," Ginger said.

We weren't that lucky.

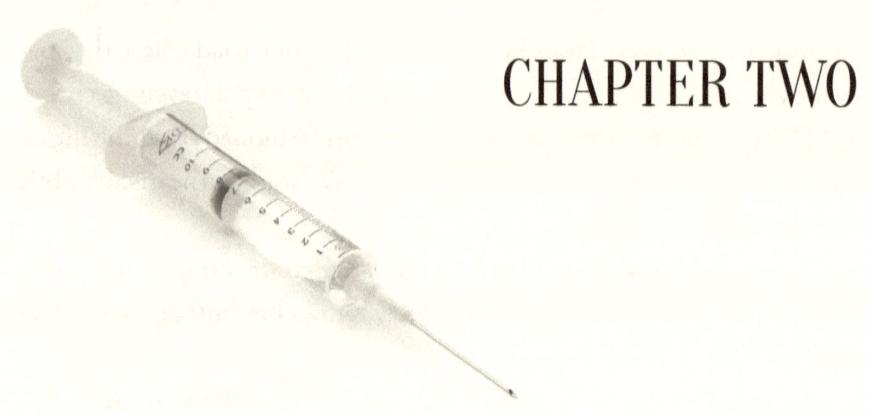

CHAPTER TWO

ndi passed out our vegetable plates and offered each of us a slice of the to-die-for cornbread. After saying a blessing, we dug into our food like we hadn't eaten in a month. The next few minutes were spent in companionable silence as we savored the delectable flavors. Appetites sated, we discussed our next decorating job. I was describing a Tiffany lamp reproduction I'd seen when I looked up to see Joan Smith standing by our table.

"Don't think I won't follow through with my threat to keep you out of the club. We don't need your kind worming their way in." Joan continued, digging in a little deeper. She turned to her companion, "This is the hussy that had an affair with Daniel."

Ginger had all the understanding she could stomach. She jumped up, "I've had just about enough of your mouth. I'm sorry your husband cheated on you, but you don't have to take it out on me. I *said* I was sorry."

Without missing a beat, Joan stared straight into Ginger's eyes and threw a verbal sucker punch, "You're sorry all right."

I saw it coming, but the hand is quicker than the eye. Ginger grabbed her half glass of iced tea and doused Joan. Tea dribbled down her platinum bob and a lemon wedge balanced precariously over one eyebrow. A river of tea poured down her beak and she sputtered, eyes wide in surprise.

Honey let out a guffaw, and I bit my tongue to keep from laughing out loud at the sight.

With mouth agape, she glared at Ginger before being swept away by one of the managers who had run over to investigate the commotion.

There was no explaining this away, so we asked for to-go boxes and made a quick get-away. When we entered the safety of my car, Ginger released her pent-up emotions and sobbed.

"Aw, sugar, don't worry. That tea will come right out of her clothes." Honey shot me a bewildered look and mouthed something I didn't catch. "That sure was quick thinking, though." Her tone belied the amusement we'd felt at seeing the woman get what was coming to her.

Ginger's chest heaved as she tried to talk through the sobs, "I'm so sorry. I didn't mean to embarrass y'all, but I couldn't take one more insult. I know I haven't lived the best life, but I have feelings, too."

"Of course you do," I offered, not wanting to start the car until she'd composed herself.

"Y'all are being too nice. Neither one of you would have ever dunked someone like I just did."

I thought back on some of the hijinks Honey and I had been a part of. "Don't be too sure," I told her.

"You probably don't have anyone coming up reminding you of your awful past, though." She drew in a ratchet breath. "I'm so ashamed of how I've lived. I'm beginning to see the consequences of living without Jesus in my life. I'm so thankful you've taken me under your wings." Honey passed Ginger a wad of Kleenex. She wiped her tears and blew her nose.

"Come on, buckle up, we can go to my house and we'll finish our dinner in peace and quiet."

I headed my car toward our Peachtree Street condo. Dusk had fallen by the time we arrived, and we grabbed our boxes and sat at the breakfast bar. "I know this isn't a good time to bring it up, but the club is having its annual beach party. Honey, you're going to help me with the decorations aren't you?"

"Of course, I am. It's the biggest bash of the year." Honey took a bite of cornbread. Her eyes rolled back. "Yum."

"What are y'all talking about?" Ginger hadn't lived with Honey long enough to know what all the fuss was about.

"We have sand hauled in and spread over the lawn to make it a beach party. Of course, we have to make do with the swimming pool being the ocean, but it's fun and everybody has a good time. The last big party of the summer."

Ginger clapped her hands. "Oh, that sounds wonderful. I want to go," she said.

Honey finished her cornbread and wiped her hands. "They're having something new this summer. We're also incorporating an arts and crafts festival this year. I can't wait to see how it turns out."

Ginger's eyes lit up with excitement. "Remember those homemade soaps and lotions we used to make in the mountains? I've dreamed about trying it again, but never had the time or opportunity."

Honey caught my eye and I nodded. "Sweetie, why don't we get you some supplies and try your hand at making them again? If they do well you could sell them as a sideline."

"Oh, no. I couldn't do that. That was just out of necessity. We didn't make them with exotic scents. Good old down home washing up suds is what we made."

Ginger and Honey, raised in the extreme North Georgia Mountains, lived a much simpler life than most. Both raised on farms, their families ate what they needed from the garden and made their household products. Things they did, out of the necessity to survive, were now seen as unique by millennials. If she had the right ingredients and buzzwords, Ginger's creations could be a big hit at the festival.

"Hey, maybe you could help me," Ginger suggested.

"I don't know Gin, I had enough of that growing up. The only kind of soap I want is the kind you buy at Bath and Body."

Honey laughed, but I knew growing up with little money had left an impact on her. She left the mountains as soon as possible and married into money. She'd told me many times about her fear of not having enough to meet her needs. I didn't think she'd have to worry about being without. She'd been married twice to older men, and both of them had died leaving her a wealthy woman.

"I think I'll go for it. I've been looking for a new line of work and I can do this on the side when I'm not working for Stylish Decor. I can't wait to get started."

With supper finished, I gathered up our boxes for the trash bin. "I've got a chocolate cheesecake in the fridge. Anybody want a slice?"

"Does a bear scratch its rump on a tree?" Honey's observation started a fit of giggles and I grabbed the cheesecake from the refrigerator along with some frozen strawberries from the freezer. We moved to the living room and chatted about our plans for the beach party and Ginger's booth as she grew increasingly more interested in trying her hand at the craft. Honey suggested the name, Naturals by Ginger. I covered my mouth trying to hide a yawn. I felt like I'd been ridden hard and put up wet.

"Skye, you look like you could use some rest." She turned to Ginger. "Why don't we go and let Skye get ready for Mitch. Who knows, she might wear her pink teddy tonight." This set the girls laughing again.

I got up and headed to the door. "Not to rush y'all off or anything, but here's the door. Don't let it hit you in the behind." This time *I* laughed. We hugged goodnight and the girls shot down the road in Honey's Crossfire. *Thank you God for good friends.*

I'd just finished with my bubble bath when Mitch came in. "Hi, babe. Can I warm up some leftovers for you?"

"That's all right. I picked up a hamburger. What I could really use is a good night's sleep though," he said.

We readied for bed and slipped beneath the cool sheets. As I relaxed I felt the stress of the day flow right out of my body but I let out a sigh I didn't intend to bother him with. Mitch rolled towards me, "What's wrong?"

I spent the next twenty minutes telling him about our encounter with Joan. Retelling the story conjured some bad feelings. I didn't think this thing between Joan and Ginger was over yet.

Mitch listened intently until I'd finished. "Aw, I wouldn't worry about it, Skye. Maybe this'll blow over and Joan will take her frustrations out on somebody else."

"I don't know. You weren't there to see the animosity Joan showed towards Ginger. I guess they'd never crossed paths until Ginger moved in with Honey and started running in our circle of friends." I wouldn't exactly call Joan a friend, but I'd known her for several years.

"Well, we're not going to figure this out tonight. How about we sleep on it and you might have a fresh outlook in the morning." He didn't wait for an answer before he kissed me soundly and turned over. Within minutes he snored steadily. If I wasn't the first one to go to sleep, I competed with Mitch sawing logs. I remembered seeing 12:30 on the digital clock right before I dozed off. I dreamed about a beach party with a giant, massive food fight in the lobby at the club as Honey stood on the sidelines rooting Ginger on.

How would we ever get all that sand out of the lobby?

CHAPTER THREE

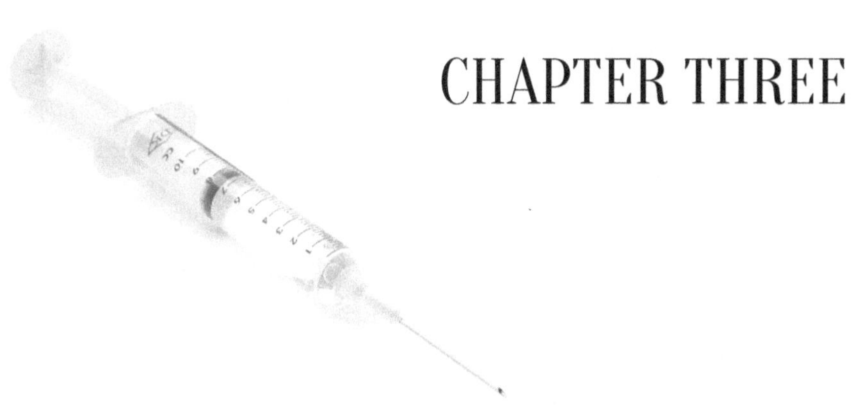

The next two weeks passed quickly. After a few trips to buy supplies and some trials that failed, Ginger succeeded in making some fairly nice natural soaps, lotions and oils to sell at the beach party. We helped by designing her labels and helped her with the packaging, and just in time for the affair. We saw to the final details of the decorations and helped her set up her booth.

The summer sun, already high, warmed the earth. A sure sign of a scorcher day – great for an outdoor party. I'd spent the previous afternoon supervising the trucks dropping several tons of sand for the annual end-of-summer shindig.

"Would you look at this?" Ginger did a three-sixty taking in the sight. "This is great. I can have fun and make some money, too." I was pleasantly surprised in the change that had taken place in Ginger's life during the short time she'd been with Honey. Yeah, she had some growing to do, but didn't we all? I'd witnessed her take the bull by the horns and let go of her old life as she replaced bad decisions with better choices.

"Yeah, it feels like we're at Tybee," Honey noted. I left them to finish the details on Ginger's booth and display her products while I made sure all the decorations were perfect for the bash.

While I walked the property, Joan kept making unwanted appearances in my mind. What if she made a scene again today? I smiled remembering the tea dripping down her nose. Perhaps we just needed to arm Ginger with her beverage weapon of choice.

When I arrived back at the booth, the girls were putting the finishing touches on the display.

"Hey, let's go over there and get some cold lemonade." Honey pointed to a booth down the row of colorful tents. We followed her over, knowing we had several minutes before the official opening.

The guy behind the booth waggled his eyebrows, "How can I help you pretty ladies?" Honey waggled her eyebrows right back. "We'll take some lemonade, John. Does Sally know you're out here flirting with all the ladies?"

John Myers' deep laugh rumbled. "No, she doesn't, and you'd better not tell her either. What happens on the beach stays on the beach." He glanced at me, "By the way, where is that husband of yours? I'll bet he'd be proud of you for transforming this place into a day at the beach."

"Why thank you. He'll be here later. We came early to help Honey's cousin set up her booth." I introduced them. "Everything Ginger makes is natural and organic."

"Good marketing, Skye," Honey said.

"You two are the best," Ginger said, sipping her lemonade noisily.

By the time we returned to the tent, people had already gathered to look at Ginger's homemade products. They picked up bars of soap, turned them over in their hands, and sniffed. Lavender seemed to be the most popular scent. By lunchtime, she'd sold more than half of what she'd brought. I predicted she'd sell out before the day ended. I met up with Mitch, and we decided on hot dogs for lunch. It was fun sitting at the picnic tables, on the make-believe beach. It made me sad to think autumn was right around the corner.

"What ya thinking about, babe?"

I pointed to the corner of my mouth alerting Mitch he had a bit of stray mustard. He wiped it off and took another bite of his slaw dog.

"Just thinking of how fast summer goes by. Especially the older I get," I said.

Honey came up and interrupted any further conversation. "Hey, guess who bought some products from Ginger?"

"I don't know. Spit it out, Honey."

"Daniel Smith. Can you believe it? Boy, I bet Joan will have a fit if she discovers where her lotion came from. Well, that is, if he bought it for her." She shook her head. "You could have knocked me over with a feather. But, I must admit, Ginger handled the situation like a pro. He didn't let on he recognized her, so she went along with the charade. I'm really proud of her."

She looked at my half-eaten hot dog. "It is lunch time. I'll grab Ginger and me a couple of dogs and head on back to the booth. You coming over after while? I could use a break and I'd love to run around with Robert."

I looked at Mitch. "What do you think? Can you keep yourself busy so I can relieve Honey?"

"Actually, I wouldn't mind getting in nine holes while you're working. I've had my fill of sand." He brushed the clinging grains off his leg to prove his point.

I spent the rest of the afternoon helping the girls. Like I'd expected, Ginger sold out of products. She had a great idea when she decided to sell natural items and it would be a good side-line for her. I'd appreciated Ginger's help at Stylish Décor, but our goal had been to build her confidence and guide her to self-reliance. We dismantled the tent and left to relax by the pool. I'd nodded off when I heard Ginger squeal.

I shot up, turned over the lounge chair and landed in the sand. "What is it?"

Ginger pointed, "Look who's coming!"

Honey and I looked in the direction where she pointed. "Uh oh," Honey said. "Here comes trouble with a capital T."

Joan strolled toward us flanked by two women in tennis skirts. One of them I recognized as Penny Marshall. What was Joan up to? She didn't waste any time revealing her intentions.

Joan kept her distance. "You were warned, Ginger. Enjoy yourself, because after today you won't be allowed on club property."

Honey stepped between Ginger and Joan. "Give it a rest, Joan. You've made your point."

Ginger stuck her head around Honey, "Joan, you look thirsty. Want another glass of iced tea?"

Joan flushed red and glanced at Penny, who leaned in to whisper something in her ear.

"You haven't heard the end of this." Joan and her clones left in a huff.

Ginger shouted after them, "You've got that right! It ain't over yet!" Ginger kicked at the sand. "I blew my new image didn't I? But no one should be pushed around by a bully."

We rounded up Mitch and headed home. Tired to the bone, I couldn't wait to soak in a warm bath. I might just wear that pink teddy Honey had bought me.

CHAPTER FOUR

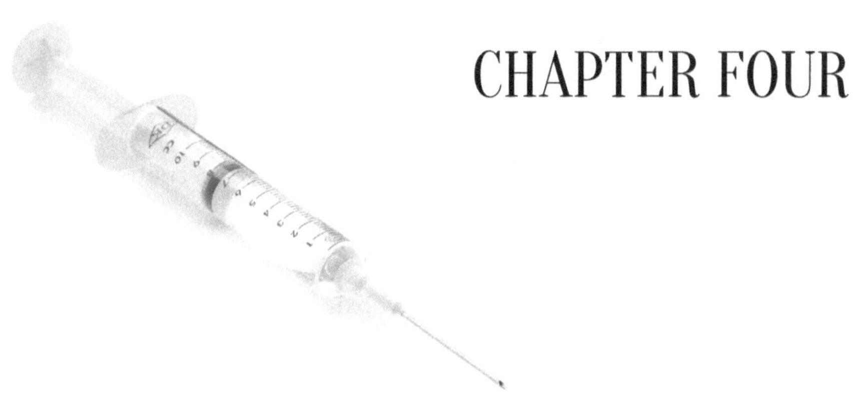

It'd been several weeks since the beach party and Ginger's new business had taken off. People who bought her products at the festival were calling and asking for more. They sold as fast as she made them. Happy for her, I imagined this as a new career for Ginger. I had two jobs in progress and a new one coming up on an historic house on Candler. Gin assured me she could still work part-time.

I'd gotten used to her being around. I had discovered sometimes the cover doesn't reflect what's on the inside. I still had a way to go, but I prayed I'd become less judgmental of those different from me. Even Isaiah said of Jesus, "He had no beauty or majesty to attract us to him, nothing in his appearance that we should desire him." The outside wrapper was not important.

Growing up, my mother greatly influenced my attitudes. We were middle class and though we never wanted for anything we weren't super rich, but Mother longed to associate with the upper echelon of Atlanta. She begged Daddy to join the country club so she could hang out with her circle of friends. She always worried about how my brother, sister and I appeared to others. The vessel mattered to her.

I grew up basing my opinions of others, as well as myself, on outward appearances. I'd tried to work on this through the years, but hadn't made much progress until I grew to know Ginger up close and personal. She might be considered a redneck hillbilly by some, but she possessed one of the most generous hearts I'd ever seen and I was thankful she'd come into my life.

The three of us were meeting to discuss the house on Candler at The Flying Biscuit, one of our favorite breakfast haunts. I spotted Honey and Ginger across the parking lot and gave them a wave. Honey had on bright orange leggings paired with a long hand-embroidered shirt embellished with orange flowers. She wore jeweled Yellow Box flip-flops and carried an orange clutch. Ginger had on skinny jeans matched up with a lime green tee. A little low cut, it showed off the girls more than necessary, but I knew as she made changes in her life, changes in her dress would follow. One step at a time.

"Hi, Skye, how ya doing this morning?" Ginger lifted her sunglasses and planted them on her head.

"Doing great. How about you girls?" I spotted an empty table and hurried to claim it. They followed close behind.

"Wow, haven't seen you move that fast in quite a while," Ginger said. No sooner had we sat down than our waitress appeared. We each ordered our favorites and sat back to discuss the new job.

The historic house in Decatur had been damaged in a storm. Since the owner, Martin McGuire, was out of the country the realtor had been given permission to have it repaired before he returned. Decatur had turned into an urban renewal community, making property in high demand. Once the home was repaired it would be put back on the market. Decatur's need for property had been a boon for business at Stylish Decor.

After we took an initial look at the house we spent the rest of the day working at the shop.

Mitch and I had made a date to eat supper together. We rarely had the opportunity to meet early. We enjoyed a quiet evening and went to bed with the chickens. I slept peacefully when the shrill of the landline shattered my sleep. I sat up faster than a bolt of lightning. A call in the middle of the night was never a good thing.

"Hello," I said breathlessly.

Honey's voice shrieked through the phone. "Oh Skye, the most terrible thing's happened."

By this time Mitch had sat up. He asked me who was on the phone. "It's Honey," I told him.

"Honey, what is it? What's wrong? Are you hurt?"

"No, it's not me. It's Ginger. She's been taken in for questioning," Honey sobbed.

"Questioning for what? I don't understand." I shook my head trying to clear the cobwebs of confusion. Mitch looked at me with wide eyes.

"They found Joan Smith dead and they're questioning Ginger. They wouldn't tell me anything other than they were taking her to the Decatur police station. What are we going to do?"

I didn't know why she asked *me* what we were going to do. Her guess was as good as mine. "Why don't I come get you and we'll go to the station and find out what's going on?"

"Oh, that would be great!"

"I'll be there in a flash."

"Hurry!"

I turned to Mitch. "That was Honey. Joan Smith was found dead and they've taken Ginger in for questioning. Honey's beside herself with worry." I knew Mitch wasn't going to be happy with me.

His pinched face said it all. "Skye, you know what happened last time you got involved in a murder investigation. You almost lost your life." His look softened, "I don't know what I'd do if anything happened to you."

I laid my hand on his arm. "We're just going to the police station in Decatur to find out what's going on. I promise we won't do anything dangerous."

Mitch rolled his eyes. "Danger seems to follow you wherever you go."

I drove to Honey's faster than I intended, but I was as anxious as Honey to vouch for Ginger. My mind swirled with unanswered questions. Was

Joan murdered? It wouldn't be a far stretch to think someone had it in for her. She wasn't the easiest person to get along with. Her life with Daniel had been one of turmoil and she took it out on anyone who got too close. Ginger might have had words with her, but she'd never harm her. Would she?

Honey already waited outside for me. Illumination from the car's dome light revealed she'd taken time to apply make-up and her signature Merle Norman Romance Red lipstick. Why was I not surprised? "I thought you'd never get here. I'm a wreck."

She turned to me and clicked on her seat belt, and said aloud what I already thought. "You don't think Ginger . . ."

"No. She couldn't. She wouldn't. Would she?"

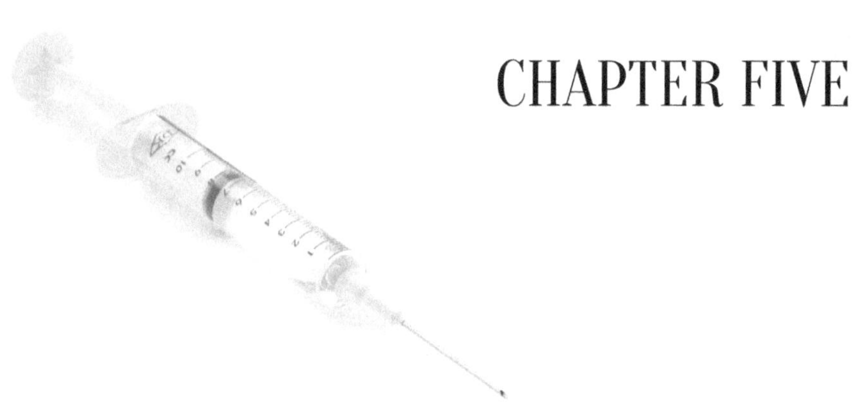

CHAPTER FIVE

With light, middle-of-the-night traffic we made good time. Honey opened the door before the car came to a complete stop. I parked, jumped out and followed her. We trailed behind a uniformed officer who had a firm grip on a handcuffed dude. What had the young man done to get into such a position?

Honey marched straight up to the desk and gave the officer sitting there the once-over. "Officer Owens, we're here to find out about my cousin, Ginger Walker. Where is she?"

He checked her up and down, looked at me, and turned back to his computer monitor. I assumed he was entering her name into the system. "She's with Detective Haynes right now." He turned to the officer with the suspect in custody, and buzzed them through a locked door. "That yer DUI?" He nodded to Honey, who still stood over him. "Why don't you take a seat over there," he pointed to a row of seats against the wall, "and wait on her?" He returned to his monitor, dismissing us.

I gently tugged on Honey's arm. "Come on. Let's sit. We're here now and that's the main thing." I led her to the faded blue chairs. I hesitated, sure they'd seen better days and a lot of rumps.

"Eww, those look nasty," Honey said.

"Yeah, but we don't have much of a choice. Let's just grin and bear it."

Honey slapped at the seat like she could eradicate any germs with the swipe of her hand. "I don't understand. One minute we were sound asleep and the next someone was banging on the door. A couple of officers swooped in and took Ginger without so much as an explanation." Honey placed her head in her hands.

We sat alone, with our thoughts for company, the next few minutes. I heard the familiar voice before I saw her. "Are you going to question me again?" A giant of a man followed Ginger. With the build of a football player he reminded me of Smokey Bear. Sweat beaded on his mahogany forehead.

Ginger noticed us and hurried over. She drew Honey into a big hug. "Oh, Honey, they kept questioning me about Joan. I tried to tell them I didn't even know her that well. I don't think Detective Haynes believed me."

I reached over and hugged Ginger, too.

Detective Haynes walked to where we huddled. "Ms. Walker, you're free to go now, but don't leave town until we let you know."

Honey let go of Ginger and turned to the detective. "What's going on here? Why did you barge into my house and kidnap my cousin?" Ginger and I emitted a collective gasp. Only five-foot-two-inch Honey would dare confront a giant of a detective. A lot of vim and vigor was packed into the small package I called my best friend.

I had to give Detective Haynes credit for keeping his cool. "Ma'am, if Ms. Walker wants to tell you what went on behind closed doors it's her choice. But you won't hear it from me. Good night." He nodded and returned to his office.

Honey and I jumped on Ginger like a duck on a Junebug. "What did he say? Do you need a lawyer? Was Joan really murdered?"

"Whoa, y'all. Wait until we get in the car and I'll tell you what happened." We hurried to the car where I beat Honey behind the wheel. I didn't trust Honey to drive safely in her present state. She sat in the back allowing Ginger to ride up front.

"I'm about to bust my britches wondering what happened in there," Honey said. "I was worried they'd arrest you." I heard Honey sniffling in the back seat. I imagined her mascara running down her tear-streaked cheeks.

"I was, too. I think they were planning on it, but after questioning me Detective Haynes said they didn't have enough to hold me. He said Joan was found dead and it had come to their attention we had a little run-in at the club and the OK Café. He asked me all kinds of personal questions about my past relationship with Daniel. I was so embarrassed." She paused for a few seconds. Silence engulfed the car. "I told him I didn't know he was married at the time and I sure didn't know Joan before the other day. I don't think he believed me."

"Ginger, I'm so sorry. It must have been terrible," I said.

"Yeah, he kept asking me the same questions over and over. I thought he'd never let me go."

I heard Honey's seatbelt unbuckle. She scooted up and laid a hand on Ginger's shoulder. "Well, you're with us now so you can relax. Let's go home and get some rest."

"Why don't y'all come on over and spend the night with me and Mitch? I'm sure he wouldn't mind." I knew he'd treat them with nothing but kindness. Mitch had said more than once, since I'd become friends with Honey I'd gotten into more trouble than the whole time he'd known me. I had to admit, since Honey, and now Ginger, had come into my life, I lived life to the fullest. I needed them as much as they needed me.

Ginger turned to Honey. "Want to?"

"Sure. We could use the support. Let's swing by the house and check on Sam and get a change of clothes for tomorrow." After checking on Samantha, Honey's Yorkie, it was almost morning by the time we arrived home. Mitch sat at the table drinking coffee when we trooped in. His eyes grew wide at the sight of the girls, but to his credit he didn't say a word about me bringing them home.

"What happened? Is everything okay now?"

I filled him in on the details.

Mitch grabbed three cups from the cabinet and filled them with coffee. "What happened to Joan?"

"She's dead," I told him, sinking into a chair. "I never really liked her that much, but I never wanted her dead." I looked at the others. "Who would want to murder her?"

We all looked at Ginger.

"Don't look at me!" she cried. "All I ever did was try to stay away from her. Except for the whole iced tea down her blouse thing and all."

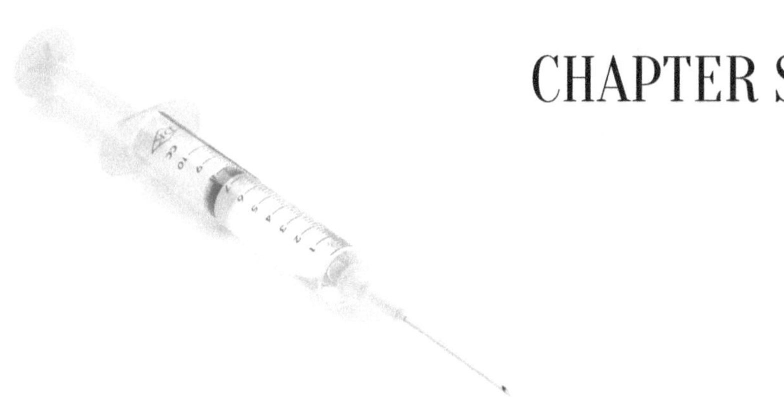

CHAPTER SIX

"They didn't tell me much about what happened. They kept questioning me about our run-ins at the club." Ginger shook her head and took a sip of coffee.

"Well, that *is* plum crazy. Those didn't mean anything. That detective didn't look too smart to me. I think I'll call Robert and see if he can help, but first I'm going to lie down before I fall down," Honey said.

Feeling like I could go to sleep in my coffee, I agreed with Honey we needed to get some rest. Mitch kissed me goodbye. I kissed him back and assured him everything would be fine, but I wasn't so sure. When he reached the door he turned, hesitated, and said, "Call me if you need me."

Before I went to sleep, my thoughts turned to the girls. Anything Honey, and now Ginger, went through, I'd be there for them. I knew the same would be true if I needed them.

It was past noon when I woke. The sun shone brightly through the blinds, promising to be another sweltering Georgia day. I looked forward to the low humidity and cool breezes of fall weather. I took a quick shower, put on clean jeans and a pullover top. By the time I finished, Ginger and Honey were up.

"You girls look like you've lost your last friend," I said.

"The news of Joan's death and Ginger's questioning is enough to put anybody in a sour mood," Honey said. "I called Robert and he said we shouldn't be too concerned, and that it would be normal to question people who had recent contact with Joan." She shook her head. "I'm not so sure, though."

The landline's shrill ring shot through the air. I picked it up. "Hello."

"Hi, hon. Just calling to see if you were up and how everything was going."

I told him Robert's advice. "It's all well and good to try and not worry, but I think we need a diversion to keep our minds off last night."

"Why don't y'all take a day off and do something fun? Anyway, I plan to be home in time for supper tonight." We talked a few more minutes before saying good-bye.

I took Mitch's recommendation to heart and suggested to the girls we take the day off. You'd have thought they'd won the lottery. Was I really that much of a taskmaster? We decided to make a day of it at Stone Mountain. Down the road, off Stone Mountain Freeway, was one of Georgia's premier tourist spots and one of my favorite places to spend an afternoon.

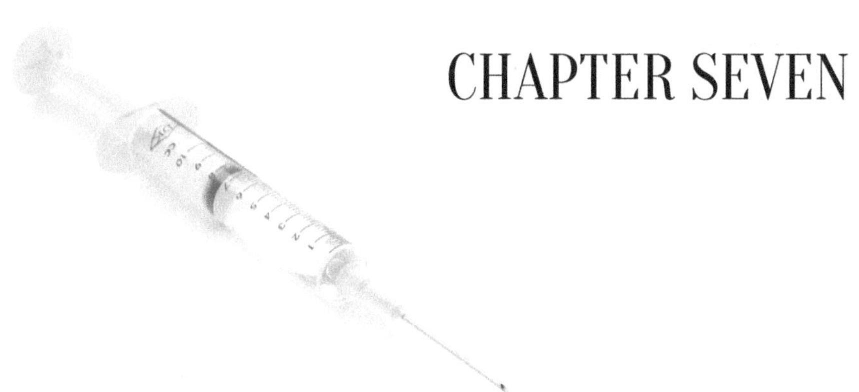

<h1 style="text-align:right">CHAPTER SEVEN</h1>

Since it was a weekday and in the early afternoon, the park wasn't as crowded as I'd seen it in the past. With some schools starting in August, most of kids had returned to the classroom.

We purchased our tickets and sat to study the brochure. No way could we do everything in one day, there were so many choices. "Hey let's play the Great Locomotive Chase putt-putt golf," Ginger said.

"Sounds like a great place to start," Honey agreed. We walked quite a way to get to the golf course. By the time we arrived, sweat was running down my shirt. The humidity made me sweat like a farm hand, but I was determined to have a good time despite the heat.

"Look! There it is." How Ginger managed to run in this heat I'd never know. Even more surprising was the fact her Tammy Faye make-up was still in place when I arrived at the ticket booth.

"Whew," I wiped the sweat from my forehead, "this heat is going to be the death of me." Honey and Ginger gave me a look that could melt ice. "What?"

"Let's don't talk about death today," Honey said.

"Oh, yeah. Bad choice of words. Sorry about that." We got our clubs from the kids running the venue. I was taking aim when the Scenic Railroad train rolled by and blew its whistle. Startled, I hit the ball and it rolled down the carpeted track and jumped over the side. Ginger and

Honey doubled over in laughter. I could have gotten mad, but it wouldn't have made any difference so I joined in.

"I'm glad you're having so much fun at my expense."

"I'm sorry, Skye, but you should have seen the look on your face." Honey put her arm around my shoulder. "It startled me, too, but when you hit that ball and it jumped the rail it was too funny." Honey started another round of teasing.

A group of senior ladies were in line to go next. One of them approached us. "If you don't mind, we don't have a lot of time. Could y'all finish up your turn?"

"Yes, ma'am." Admonished, I went to retrieve my ball.

I heard Honey talking to Ginger as I strolled away. "Well, she's got that right. She doesn't have much time."

I shouldn't have, but a little laugh escaped my lips. Honey was a spitfire. There was never a dull moment with her around.

We finished the game and Ginger came in first. I came in second and Honey brought up the rear. We enjoyed ourselves so much we'd almost forgotten about poor Joan.

That was until Detective Montaine a.k.a., Robert, called Honey with killer news. I could tell it wasn't good when her face turned as white as a southern Magnolia blossom.

"What is it Honey?" Ginger asked just above a whisper. She grabbed Honey's arm and gave it a shake as her voice grew louder. "Come on, tell us. You look like your best friend just died."

She turned to Ginger. "No. But that's how I feel. That was Robert and he was letting me know they want to question you again." Now Ginger turned white.

"Why, because we had a couple of heated discussions? That's ludicrous." She stomped her foot. Ginger's fear had turned to indignation in a matter of minutes. "I did not kill Joan Smith!"

"I can't believe this is happening." Honey and I were suspects in a murder just months before. What were the chances Ginger had now become a murder suspect? A gazillion to one? "What's going to happen now?"

Honey's answer was barely audible.

"Speak up, Honey, I didn't hear what you said."

Honey spoke up all right – she nearly shouted, "I said, they want her for questioning." There was a collective gasp from the group of senior ladies. We'd been so upset; we'd forgotten there were other people around.

Honey, Ginger's staunch defender, stared at the group. "What are y'all looking at?" They turned around and chattered among themselves. I easily imagined what they were saying – and it wasn't good.

"Honey, that's not like you to be so rude."

She lowered her head, "I'm sorry, but I'm so rattled I don't even know what I'm saying." She turned to me and asked, "What are we going to do?" Like I had all the answers.

Ginger swiped at tears running down her cheeks. "I don't want to go to jail. They don't even allow you to wear make-up in jail."

Well, that's as good a reason to stay out of jail if I ever heard one. "Don't worry, Ginger. Honey and I have your back. But for now, I think we should do what Robert suggests. Maybe we should look into hiring a lawyer."

"No," Ginger said, "that would imply I'm guilty."

Honey agreed. "I think she's right. Come on, Ginger, we'll show 'em."

We arrived at the station with confidence this was all a big mistake and would be cleared up soon. The officer on night shift had been replaced. Officer Donna sat behind the desk. We'd met her when Sylvia Landmark had been murdered and we'd been questioned at the Buckhead police station on more than one occasion. She must have been transferred to the Decatur precinct. I wouldn't be surprised if Donna didn't think we'd done the dirty deed.

She looked up with a smile on her face. It faded quickly. "Well, who do we have here? The three musketeers?" She addressed Honey next, "Robert's not here, ya know."

Honey clenched her fists, but spoke calmly. "We're not here to see him. We want to talk to Detective Haynes."

"Well, take a seat and I'll let him know you're here." She picked up the phone, I assumed, to apprise him of our presence.

Honey grabbed a wad of napkins from her purse and wiped off her seat. "Yuck! I hate these chairs. I'll have to talk to Robert about getting new ones."

Ginger sniffed, "Honey, why can't I talk to Robert? I don't want to talk with Detective Haynes."

"Robert said he couldn't take part in the investigation because we'd been dating, plus it's not in his district. I'm sorry."

Ginger didn't have time to respond. Footsteps preceded the detective. The man with an indomitable presence motioned for us to come on back.

He put his hand up, palm out. "No, not all three of you." He pointed to Ginger. "Just her."

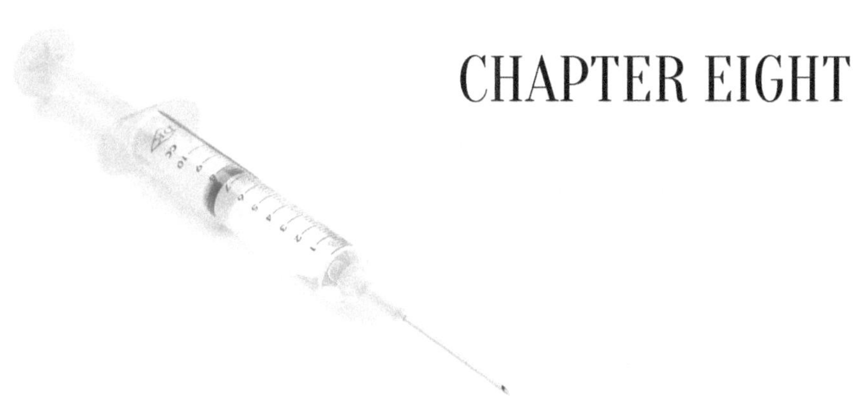

CHAPTER EIGHT

Over an hour had passed since Ginger had gone to the detective's office. Honey, who'd been pacing back and forth for the last twenty minutes, stopped in front of Officer Donna's desk. "When is he going to let her go?"

Officer Donna slowly looked up from her work. "I don't know. When they finish?"

"Humph!" Honey's jaw clenched and her face flushed.

It would be another hour before Ginger and Detective Haynes came out. Ginger's swollen eyes and streaked mascara gave testament to an intense session. I knew from watching real life mysteries on TV, detectives could be relentless. Their theory being, the longer they kept you the more apt you were to break and spill your guts. But I knew Ginger didn't have anything to spill.

Honey jumped up and ran to meet a beleaguered Ginger. She embraced her shoulder and led her to the seats. Honey turned to Detective Haynes. "How could you? I know what you're doing. Trying to get her to confess to something she didn't do. You wait until I tell Robert."

Oh, boy, I was sure Robert would never live this one down with the boys at the station. I decided to take over before Honey made it worse. "Honey, come on. Let's get Ginger home."

She turned her back on the detective. "Come on, sugar, let's go."

"Not so fast," said Ginger's torturer. "Ms. Walker, don't leave the area. I'll be getting back with you." He didn't stop there, "Ms. Southerland and Ms. Truelove, I need to talk with y'all, too. Make an appointment for tomorrow if you would, please."

Stern, but polite, he was the epitome of a southern gentleman. I knew he was doing his job, but I couldn't help but feel resentment for what he'd put Ginger through. He turned and sauntered toward his office. I told Honey to take Ginger out to the car while I made our appointments. He wanted to talk to us separately so we had back-to-back times. I knew he'd ask about the incident at the country club, and I dreaded telling him what I'd witnessed. It didn't put Ginger in a good light.

When I got in the car, the girls were discussing the interview. "That's the most ridiculous thing I've heard," Honey said. "There's no way your products are pertinent to the case."

I turned towards Ginger, dying to hear what I'd missed.

"He didn't say they were, he said it proved I'd had recent contact with Daniel since he bought them."

Ginger continued. "Sure, I was mad she embarrassed me at the club and called me a hussy, but why'd I want to kill her?"

"I think they must not have any good leads on who really did kill Joan," I said. I shook my head.

"Well, don't you worry, Ginger. I know if we have faith the truth will come out. Isn't that right, Skye?"

"That's right." I believed in her innocence, but did I believe in the system? If Honey and I were wrongly accused, it could happen to anyone. But if the girls could have faith, so could I. I said a little prayer right then and there, "*Lord, please help Ginger out of this mess.*"

"Y'all want to come back over for another night?"

"No, thank you." Ginger sounded weary. She had just begun to realize there was a better way to make a living than being an exotic dancer. She had been excited about future possibilities, now she was a suspect in a murder case. "I just want to go crawl into my bed. But thanks Skye."

Secretly, I was relieved to be headed for a quiet evening with my husband. By the time I arrived home, Mitch had cooked supper for the two of us. He looked behind me to see if I had brought any strays home. A big grin spread across his face. "Have a nice day playing hooky?"

"Oh, Mitch, you won't believe what happened." His eyebrows raised in question. "We were on the tenth hole; you know the one with the impossible loop-de-loop? Robert called Honey and told her they wanted to question Ginger again. They kept her more than two hours."

"That doesn't sound good." Mitch took my hand and pulled me into the dining room. He'd set the table with good china and had lit the candles. A colorful gift bag sat beside my plate.

I searched my brain to figure out if I'd missed an anniversary or something. "What did I do to deserve the royal treatment?" It felt good to be pampered. Lately, Mitch and I had been working late hours and didn't spend nearly enough time together. This must be his way of telling me he wanted me all to himself tonight.

I couldn't wait to open my gift, imagining some exotic perfume or bath salts, or hoping it was a sparkling piece of new jewelry. I took out the pink crepe paper and withdrew – a Taser?

"It could save your life someday. Tell me if I'm wrong, but if Ginger isn't exonerated you'll start snooping around trying to help her."

I couldn't disagree, and once I recovered from my shock, I threw my arms around his neck. Mitch knew me too well. And what's more, he really cared about my safety. More important than any bling in my book.

He laid his hand over mine. "Promise me you'll carry it when you go out."

"Of, course, I will."

After our delicious dinner, I spent the night cuddled next to Mitch. I slept so soundly until morning I barely heard him dressing, and didn't even hear him leave for work. I wiped the sleep from my eyes and stumbled to the kitchen. I'd no sooner sat down to coffee and a pastry when the phone rang.

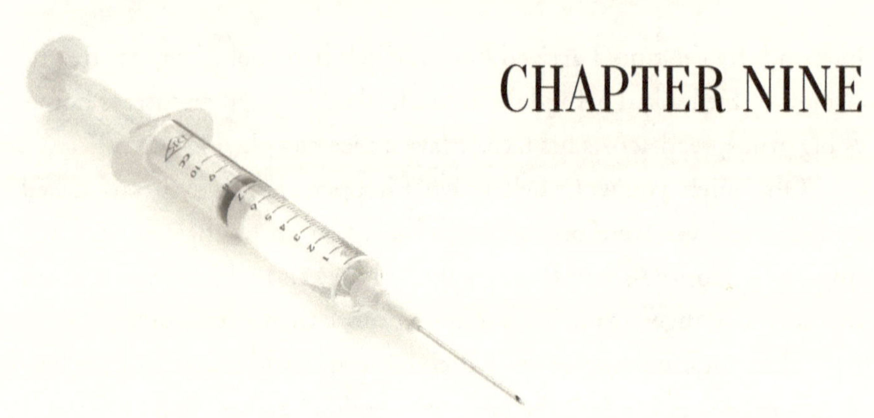

CHAPTER NINE

"Hi, Honey."

"Checking the caller ID again?"

"Well, I am particular about who I talk to. How's Ginger doing this morning?" I was pretty sure she wasn't doing too well.

"Glad I made the cut." I heard Honey sigh. "Well, we stayed up late talking and we even prayed about it. She felt a little better when we went to bed. She's still asleep. What do you think is going to happen, Skye?"

"I don't know. If she doesn't want a lawyer yet, I guess we need to sit tight for now. What did Robert say?" Honey and the detective had gotten closer over the past few months. I hoped it would bloom into a full-blown relationship. Honey had been lonely since her late husband, Frank, had died. She had a new spring in her step that hadn't been there in quite a while. "Do y'all feel like working today?"

"I do. I think it would do Ginger good to keep her mind occupied. I'll let her sleep another thirty minutes and then I'll get her up. I think we can be at the shop by ten. Would that be all right?"

"That'll work. Remember, we're taking inventory the next couple of days and I have a meeting with the architect to discuss the repair work on the old Candler Street house. Why don't y'all come with me? It's at four and by the time we finish it'll be time to eat. I've a hankering for a veggie burger from the Brick Store and we'd be in the area."

"Sounds good. I'd better hang up if we're going to make it by ten. I'll see you later. And, Skye? I want you to know how much I appreciate you stepping up and helping me with Ginger's rehab. But I never in a million years thought we'd be dealing with murder charges."

"We'll get through it if we stick together. We've already proven that. I'll see you at ten." We said goodbye and I took a quick shower and threw on some khakis and a teal short sleeve tee. I'd taken to splashing some color into my wardrobe lately. I found a hot pink and teal scarf, put on my Dockers and headed out the door.

I got in my trusty Highlander and headed to work. With little traffic, the going was smooth sailing. I reached the store in twenty minutes. It wasn't time for Honey and Ginger to arrive so with everything that had happened to us in the past few days swirling in my brain, I began taking inventory, so I nearly dropped a sample book when Honey startled me.

"Hi Skye!"

I narrowed my eyes, "You snuck up on me."

"I most certainly did not, you were lost in thought again." Honey stood, one hand on her hip. A familiar pose.

I looked beyond Honey and caught a glimpse of Ginger. Something about her was changed. Her makeup was lighter, subtler, making her look several years younger.

"You look well rested this morning, Ginger. I hope you slept okay."

"Thanks, Skye, I feel better. Honey prayed with me before bed, and I'm sure before long they will find the real killer."

"Well, you're probably right." I had a million thoughts galloping through my mind. "How about you girls taking the other room while I finish up here? We have a meeting with Gabby Miller this afternoon and I want to get this chore behind us first."

Ginger grabbed a notebook and pen from my desk. "Honey mentioned we're going to the Brick Store today. I love going to the Square, but I've never been there to eat." Ginger was tall, but slim. At least her appetite seemed all right.

I was a lone wolf in this pack when it came to putting on the pounds. I could gain five pounds by looking at a piece of pie. Not the girls. They pretty much ate what they wanted and didn't gain an ounce. With them being cousins it must be in their genes.

"That's settled so let's get busy. There's a possibility we could finish today if we don't get distracted." We worked right through lunch. Our diligence paid off when we finished with just enough time to reach Candler.

We loaded the back of the Highlander and headed out to meet with Gabby, glad the whole problem of Joan's death was behind us.

At least I hoped it was.

Ginger took shotgun this time. "Is Gabby short for Gabriela?"

"Yes, I believe it is."

I was on West Bankhead Highway when I spotted my exit. I swerved into the right lane barely making the exit. Honey squealed in the back. "Are you trying to get us killed? That car almost hit us."

"Yeah, but it didn't. Anyway, you say the same thing every time we get on a four lane and I haven't killed us yet."

CHAPTER TEN

I pulled into the drive of the two-story Victorian house. The outside needed some tender loving care, but was in fairly good shape. I couldn't wait to see what the inside looked like.

Gabby offered us a wave from the front porch. "Oh, she's not as old as I thought she'd be," Ginger said. "She's the owner isn't she?"

"No, she's the architect. I thought you knew."

"I heard you talk about meeting the architect and then we talked about Gabriela. I didn't put the two together. I never dreamed the architect would be a girl. Where I come from girls got married and had babies. Or vice versa."

Honey had told me many times they didn't have much and they weren't encouraged to succeed in school. Attending college was out of the question.

"I don't suppose you've heard of Leila Wilburn?"

Ginger shook her head.

"She was the first woman architect in the Atlanta area in the early 1900's. She designed many of the homes built during that period. Many of them are still standing today. What I'm trying to say is you can be anything you want to be."

"Let's get out and meet her!" Ginger jumped out of the car and ran up to Gabby and shook her hand. "I'm so happy to meet a woman architect. You don't get to meet many of them when you're an exotic dancer." Ginger continued to pump her hand.

"Uh, nice to meet you, too." Gabby looked at me and Honey, then back at her admirer still holding her hand.

I hurried to Gabby's rescue.

"Gabby this is Ginger Walker, my assistant and Honey's cousin. We were talking about Leila Wilburn and the influence she had on housing design in Atlanta."

"Ms. Wilburn definitely influenced my being an architect." She withdrew her hand from Ginger's and extended it to Honey. "Nice to meet you, Honey. If you'll follow me inside, I can show you what repairs will be needed and what our vision is."

The screen was missing, but the rounded doorway topped with glass windows made for a grand welcome from this old house. I imagined it had seen its share of high society during the stunning house's early days. I entered, expecting the same condition as the outside. My breath hitched as if hit in the stomach.

Honey gasped. "What in the world happened in here?"

My heart sank. A giant oak tree had fallen on the back of the house. A large tarp covered the gap in the roof, but from the stench, I could tell the carpet was already ruined. And why would anyone want to cover these beautiful wood floors with carpet anyway?

I looked at Gabby. "I suppose the homeowner was heart-broken."

"It's tragic. The last storm weakened the tree and it fell over. He wants the repairs and some decorating changes done in here as soon as possible."

"It looks like we've got our work cut out for us," I said.

The rest of the house wasn't much better. We stayed about an hour discussing essential repairs. I couldn't wait to get my hands on this old beauty and make it the showplace it once was.

As we were leaving Honey picked up a picture of a middle-aged man, "Who is this? Is he someone famous?"

"He's the owner," Gabby said. "Why do you ask?"

Honey studied the photograph. "He looks familiar, that's all." She set the picture frame on the table.

Back in the car Honey scooted forward and leaned between us. "Are we still going to the Brick Store?"

"We sure are. I'm headed there now." We turned in the direction of the square onto Clairemont, ending right in front of the Decatur City Courthouse. I hooked a left and swerved into the Square parking lot. As usual, it was full. We waited a minute, hoping for a space. I started to pull away when Honey yelled.

"Skye! That car's leaving. Let's get it." Hunting for a parking space reminded me of a tiger ready to pounce. And few dare to get in front of a tiger and his prey. I know because I've attempted that feat and if looks could kill I'd be dead.

The good news was we didn't have far to walk. The restaurant was located directly across from the parking lot. Ginger gaped at the large wooden door with tree limbs for handles. "It looks like something right out of the woods."

We were seated by a young woman who handed us menus. I didn't have to look at mine. We ordered sweet tea all around. "I'll be back with your drinks in a jiffy."

"Wow, this place is great. Why haven't you brought me here before?" Ginger opened her menu.

The inside ambiance was as unique as the front door. The walls were made of brick and the rafters were a dark oak. From a small landing at the top, you could watch the activity downstairs.

Honey and I ordered veggie burgers and sweet potato chips. "You want one too, Ginger?"

She screwed up her face, "Is that one of them burgers that's made out of all vegetables?"

"Yeah, and boy is it good. I've never eaten a better one," Honey said. She patted her stomach in anticipation.

"No thank you! I'll stick with a plain ole' cow burger, please." Ginger certainly had a way with words. When she first came to stay with Honey, I cringed every time she opened her mouth, not knowing what might pop out. I'd been working on my attitude, though, and had to admit, sometimes her colloquialisms were downright funny. That's not to say I still didn't feel a twinge of embarrassment every now and then.

"Honey, I don't know what's gotten into you since you've been living in Atlanta." Ginger shook her head. "Eating a burger made out of veggies. Yew!"

"You'll never know if you like it if you don't try it."

We chatted about the house and the renovations it would need to make it viable. Before long the young waitress set our plates on the heavy wooden table. All talk stopped while we took our first bites.

We'd finished and were debating whether to get dessert when a shrill sound split the air. We all checked our phones. Ginger won the draw.

CHAPTER ELEVEN

Curious creatures that we are, it's frustrating to hear a one-sided conversation. Especially when you catch only one-syllable words. Ginger's eyes grew large as she listened. She nodded her head at something the caller said. Her eyes glazed as tears threatened to spill down her cheeks.

Honey placed an arm around Ginger's shoulder. "What's the matter, sugar?"

"It was Detective Haynes. He wants me to come in again. When is this nightmare going to end?" The tears, no longer contained, ran down her face. "He said he wants y'all to come, too."

"Uh, oh." I looked at Honey, "we forgot our appointments. He won't be happy."

"I don't think he's ever happy," Honey said.

"Come on, Ginger, let's get this over with. Don't worry, we'll be there with you." I snuck Honey a pleading look.

"Yeah, come on, sugar. No matter how many times they try to pin this murder on you we'll stick by you." We gathered our purses, paid our check and headed into unknown waters.

Honey's diatribe about the injustices of the legal system took up most of the ride to the station. She was going to put a stop to Detective Hayne's badgering. I dreaded witnessing how she was going to accomplish that feat. *Lord, you know our needs.*

The unfamiliar officer behind the desk shot us a beleaguered smile. We checked in and sat in the all too familiar seats. I wouldn't be surprised if I found our names on them. It was only a few minutes until the detective appeared. "Ms. Truelove, I'll talk to you first."

"That works out fine because I want to talk to you, too." Detective Haynes' eyebrows rose to meet his forehead. I believe he might have just met his match in this ball of fire. Honey had never been one to bridle her emotions and more than once her mouth had gotten her in trouble. I expected this to be one of those times.

He placated her with a smile. She looked at me as if to say, "Watch this! I'll wipe that smirk off his face."

"Officer, make sure you take care of these ladies. Get them a Coke or whatever." He gave a little bow and made a sweeping motion for Honey to go first.

We declined the offer for a Coke. Ginger was quiet for a few minutes before the dam broke. "Skye, I don't understand what's happening. I thought when I decided to quit being an exotic dancer my life would change and everything would be great. Now, look. I'm a murder suspect." She twisted the hem of her blouse.

"I understand. We all experience those feelings at times, but we can't give up on God. He never promised an easy life, but he promised to never leave us. I believe he's got this and the truth will come out." And I did believe the truth would be revealed. I just didn't know when and how. I guess that's where faith comes in.

She turned in her chair and looked at me, eyes wide. "You've felt that way, too? I thought you had it all together. You've got a nice business, an apartment, and Mitch. You have it all."

Ginger hit a nerve. Yes, it would appear to others I possessed everything. But my heart ached for the one thing I couldn't have. "I'm going to share something with you I rarely talk about. It's quite personal, and painful at times."

"What's that?" Ginger sat up a little, her interest peaked.

"I've wanted children since Mitch and I were married. I prayed, pleaded and begged God to let me be a mother. When it didn't happen, I blamed him. There were times when I couldn't pray anything but the Lord's Prayer." A tear ran down my cheek and plopped on the back of my hand. I searched for a Kleenex. "It's been many years now and I know I'll never be able to have children, but I've found other things to fill my life. My heart still aches sometimes when I hear a newborn's cry, but I no longer blame God." I swiped the tissue under my eyes. "And remember when Honey and I were suspects a few months ago? We were exonerated of any wrong-doing."

"Yeah, but we had to do a little detecting ourselves to get y'all out of that one." She had a point.

"We'll do the same for you if we have to."

Ginger jumped up and gave me a bear hug. "Thank you so much for the pep talk. I guess everybody has problems. Even people who look like they don't."

I could hear Honey's voice from down the hallway. "Well, I'm telling you Ginger didn't do it. Just because she had an affair with Daniel doesn't mean she wanted to knock off Joan. That was a long time ago, anyway. We are going to prove her innocence." *We are?*

He ignored Honey and directed his comments to me, "Okay, Ms. Southerland, I'm ready for you."

Honey sat by Ginger. I dutifully followed Detective Haynes down the hall. He stepped aside and let me enter first. I'd been through this routine before and I didn't like it then and I was pretty sure I wouldn't like it now.

"Have a seat." He pointed to a brown vinyl chair that had seen better days. I plopped down, pleasantly surprised it had survived with a little padding. I wished Robert, a.k.a. Magnum P.I., was interviewing me. He wasn't near as intimidating as Detective Haynes. Those dark chocolate eyes bore right through me.

CHAPTER TWELVE

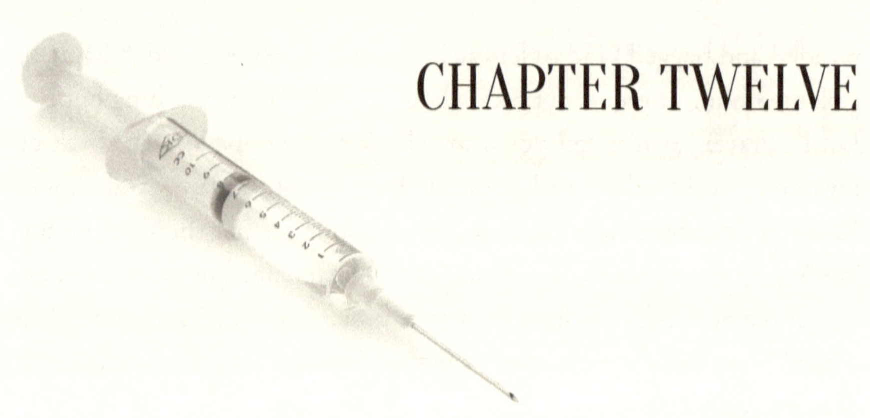

He pulled up a straight-back chair and set it directly in front of me. I was sure he'd done this same thing hundreds of times. He scooted to the edge and placed his forearms on his legs. Any closer and he'd be in my lap.

"Ms. Southerland, please tell me about the episode at the country club and later at the restaurant."

I'd been afraid he'd ask me to recount the ugly scene between Ginger and Joan. "Well, there was a little discussion between them."

"I've heard from several people and I believe there was more to it than a 'little discussion.' You might as well spill it."

I squirmed, trying to find a comfortable spot. I decided to come clean and tell the whole torrid story, even though it wouldn't paint a pretty picture for Ginger. I felt guilty, but the detective knew. I just confirmed what he'd already been told.

I looked at my phone. It'd only been forty-five minutes, but it seemed a lot longer when he told me I was free to go. I was happy to be out of the hot seat, and figured Ginger would be next.

"I need to talk with Ms. Walker, again. I expect she'll need you to stick around until she's finished. I must say the latest turn of events does not look good for her." He followed me out to the lobby where he pointed a finger at Ginger and she followed him for another turn in the hot seat. My stomach tightened like a wet knotted rope.

I took a seat next to Honey. "He said there were some new developments and it didn't look good for Gin."

"Yeah, he told me the same thing. I think he's trying to scare us," Honey said.

"Well, he succeeded with me. I guess we'll find out soon enough." I sat back and closed my eyes, wishing this would all go away.

My phone played my latest download, Mercy Me's "Flawless". I ignored it for a while, until my curiosity got the best of me. The caller ID identified Mitch. "Hello."

"Hi, hon. What are y'all up to? Keeping your nose clean?"

"Mitch, we're back at the police station with Ginger. Something's rotten in Denmark for them to keep calling her back in. I'm scared." More scared than I wanted to admit. She had so many strikes against her. Ginger's past would certainly influence their decisions. The sticky situation Ginger was now in, proved your past could certainly haunt you.

"Why don't you wait and see what happens before you fall to pieces?" "Don't worry," was easy for him to say. He hadn't been questioned by Detective Ironsides. "Anyway, we've got something more pressing to deal with."

I inhaled. "What is that?"

"I forgot to tell you I received a call from Mother a couple of weeks ago. She needs to stay with us for a week or two. They're redoing the wiring in her house."

"You what?" I rarely lost my temper with Mitch, but if he'd been in front of me I'd have given him my two cents worth. "How could you forget a visit from *Miss* Charlotte? So when's she coming? I need two or three days to prepare." I held my breath.

"That's just it, Skye. I've been so busy at work her visit slipped my mind. I'm going to pick up Mother this evening. I'm so sorry." The regret in his voice did nothing to temper my anger. I'd have to ask for forgiveness later, but for now my irritation stewed.

"Mitch, you know she's going to expect the house to be spotless and supper on the table when she arrives." Of course, she'll blame it on me. Her Mitchell, can do no wrong.

"I understand your anger, Skye, and I don't blame you. I guess I'd better go now so I can finish up here before I leave."

"You'll have to take her out for dinner. It'll be late when I get home."

I kind of felt sorry for him being on the wrong side of my wrath, but I was the one who would have to deal with his mother. Old money and old ways was the best way to describe Charlotte Southerland. Raised in Savannah, Georgia where her family could be traced back to the original settlers, Miss Charlotte never missed a chance to remind you of her heritage. Her family moved to Atlanta when she was a young lady where she'd met Mitch's father. Two families from old money married and combined their wealth. Mitch had already inherited a large amount when his father died and he stood to inherit more when Miss Charlotte passed.

She insisted I call her *Miss* Charlotte, which she pronounced without the "R." *Chalotte.* Made me feel like I was one of the help. Honey called her Lottie. For some reason she'd been taken with Honey and let her in where others were not allowed. Speaking of Honey, I'd forgotten she was there, until she shook my arm.

"Hey, what was that all about? You look like you stole the white right off a ghost." She tilted her head one way and then the other.

"Mitch informed me his mother is coming for a visit. Today!" I ran my hand through my short-cropped hair and straightened my glasses. "Can you believe Mitch forgot to tell me? What am I going to do?"

"Aw, don't worry about Lottie. I'll handle the ole' gal. You know I can wrap her around my little finger." Honey wiggled her pinky.

"Yeah, I know. I wish she felt that way about me." She constantly found fault in everything I did. I hated to admit it, but I dreaded her visit. What in the world would she think of Ginger?

"You take her too seriously, Skye. Go along with her odd ways and it'll make for smooth sailing."

It was kind of hard to find common ground when Miss Charlotte still lived in the 50's. Her daily attire consisted of a dress, high heels, pearls, and if she were going out, her little white gloves and hat. I wasn't sure why she insisted on living in the past. Was she afraid of change or did she really live in another era in her mind?

I was deep in thought when Ginger came back into the lobby with red rimmed eyes – again.

Detective Haynes followed close behind. "All right ladies, I'm finished with y'all for now." He shot a steely look at Ginger. "I'm sure we'll be needing you again, Ms. Walker. Stay handy."

She nodded. "Yes, sir." She looked deflated and defeated. Kind of the way I felt.

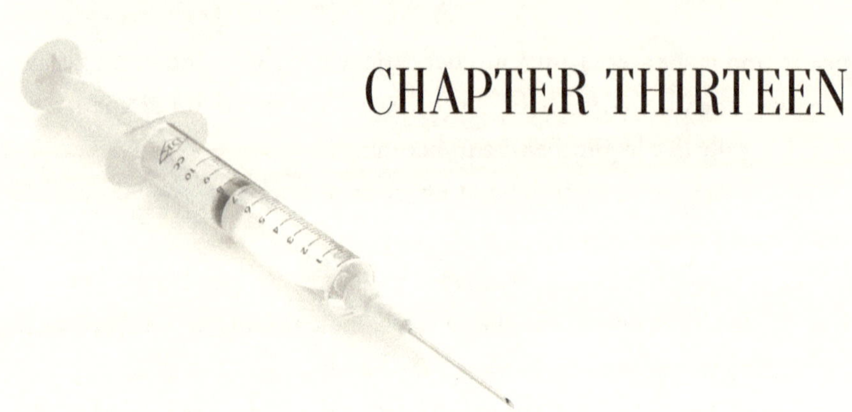

CHAPTER THIRTEEN

We traipsed out to the car where Ginger, who usually called shotgun, robotically climbed into the back seat. Honey didn't waste any time. "All right. Fill in the blanks. What are the turn of events the detective talked about that changes the play book?"

"I can't believe I'm in this nightmare. It doesn't make any sense," Ginger said.

I looked in the rear view mirror and saw her shake her head.

"He said someone poisoned her. Since I'd had an affair with Daniel in the past and my products were found at the crime scene, I'm a suspect." She reached her hand toward Honey. "Kleenex please."

"Whoa, that puts a whole different perspective on the case. Did he say what kind of poison?" This was getting more convoluted by the minute.

"Yes, but I don't remember. I remember the word organ though, but that doesn't make much sense. I personally don't know why Daniel would want to kill Joan. If anything, with his womanizing, it should be the other way around. I know I felt like killing him when I found out he was married." Ginger honked into the tissue.

"It doesn't get you off the hook, but at least they've got their focus on Daniel now," Honey said. "Maybe they'll discover he acted alone."

I threw in my opinion. "What would his motive be?"

Honey offered her two cents. "What if he framed Ginger to take the heat off him?"

Ginger inhaled. "He may have been a Romeo, but I can't believe he'd kill his wife and frame me. No! He wouldn't do that!" Ginger was adamant, but I wasn't so sure. People kill for different reasons and most of the time the perpetrator's someone close to the victim.

"I'll drop you off at the shop, Honey. Unless y'all want to come and say hi to *Miss* Charlotte." My chest constricted at the mention of her name. I'd often prayed about our relationship, but with little results. Like some mamas she didn't think I was good enough for her son. Mitch being an only child, she longed for grandchildren. That thought stung. *Lord, grant me patience.*

We pulled into the parking lot. "Here's your stop." I didn't want them to go; I needed their moral support to face Mitch's mother. I put the car in park and turned towards the girls, "Will you come over tomorrow? It's Saturday and y'all can help entertain Le Madame."

That coaxed a grin from the girls. Honey deferred to Ginger. "You feel up to it?"

"Why not, at least it'll keep my mind off being a suspect in a murder case."

"We'll see you in the morning. How about eleven?"

"That's fine. Have a good night, girls." They said goodnight and headed to Honey's Crossfire. The little red car fit Honey's personality to a tee. *A spitfire and a Crossfire.* I chuckled at the comparison despite my mood.

I arrived home, pulled up my big girl panties, and headed to the door. I knew the next two weeks would be a challenge. One, two, three, go! It started as soon as I entered.

"Well, dear, I see you worked late tonight." No, "howdy do", or "how are you"? "Mitch and I had to eat supper out, and you know what I think about restaurant food."

Of course, we all did.

"Abominable!"

I looked at Mitch. He shrugged. Since Miss Charlotte didn't mention it, I kept mum about Ginger and the fact we'd spent most of the evening at the police station.

"I'm sorry. I'll try and have a home-cooked meal tomorrow night." I wasn't sure I could pull it off, but I'd give it my best shot. Anything to escape her judgment.

"I'm tired, I think I'll turn in for the night," Miss Charlotte said, and turned to me, "I'll have breakfast at eight, dear. I want to keep on my schedule." She addressed Mitch, "You know how irregular I can get."

He grinned at me and patted his mother's arm. "Yes, Mother. We'll try our best to keep you on schedule."

The green-eyed monster reared its ugly head when she reached up and kissed Mitch on the cheek. "Good night, Skye. You shouldn't work so late; it isn't good for your marriage, dear." She went into her room and closed the door.

I wanted to be mad at Mitch, but I needed him for an ally. I would be leaning on him for support during his Mother's visit.

As Jesus said, 'whatever you did for the least of these, you did for me.' *Lord, help me remember this when dealing with Miss Charlotte.*

"Come on, babe. Let's go to bed. Things will look better in the morning." I followed him upstairs like a little puppy. It felt good to snuggle. I fell asleep saying my prayers.

My favorite song filled my dreams. No. It was my phone, and I struggled through the haze of sleep to answer it.

I glanced at the time. Seven-thirty! Cobwebs cluttered my mind. The caller ID displayed a number I didn't recognize. I hesitated a second before answering. "Hello." I looked for Mitch, but he was already gone.

"Is this Skye Southerland?"

"Yes."

"You've got to help me!"

CHAPTER FOURTEEN

I sat up, wide awake now. "Who is this?"

"Dr. Smith." He hesitated. "Daniel Smith."

"Daniel, I'm sorry about Joan." I struggled to gather my thoughts. "What do you mean I have to help you?" I knew Daniel and Joan from socializing at the club occasionally.

"I know this is going to sound crazy, but I'm in trouble." The last part ended in a catch. He paused a moment and went on. "I've been arrested for Joan's murder."

"Oh, Daniel, that's terrible." All the while my mind was spinning like a hamster on a wheel. This could be good for Ginger – take the focus off her, or perhaps make it worse since she could be implicated because she'd been close to Daniel at one time. "Why in the world are you calling me?"

"It was big news at the club, when you and Honey helped solve Sylvia Landmark's murder. I figured you could help me, too. I know it looks bad, but you've got to believe me. I didn't do it!"

I wasn't so sure about that. "The only reason we got involved in Sylvia's murder was because we were trying to save our hides. We're not professionals or anything." And it had nearly cost us our lives.

"Well, you might consider helping me since Ginger is on their radar, too. They questioned me about our past relationship. From what they said, they're going to keep a close eye on her for any involvement. It could be a win-win situation. You find the real killer, exonerate Ginger, and at the same time prove my innocence as well. They could name her as an accessory, you know."

He made a good point. I checked the clock – ten minutes until eight. Her highness would be expecting breakfast soon. "Look, Daniel, I've got to go. I'll talk to the girls and get their opinions. I need more details, though."

"My arraignment is later this morning. I hope my lawyer can get me out on bail; I don't think I'd be considered a flight risk. How 'bout I call you when they let me go. Think we could meet this afternoon?"

"I'll let you know later, but I have to go now." I disconnected without committing one way or another, threw the phone on the bedside table, and hopped out of bed. There was no way I could get dressed and have breakfast ready in a few minutes. I prepared for another lecture.

I dashed to the closet, slipped on a pair of black jeans, and matched them with a short-sleeved coral tee. I hoped the color would brighten my face, since I didn't have time to apply make-up. I finger combed my hair to add a little body and gave it a good spray. I slipped my feet into a pair of flip-flops and hurried downstairs. Too late!

"It's five after eight and I don't see my breakfast." Miss Charlotte looked around the kitchen as if bacon and eggs might be hidden behind the blender. Fashionable in a bygone era, her black dress sported a white lace collar. She had put on hose and heels. Albeit, they weren't "high" heels, but they were heels. Standing ram-rod straight she could have balanced a book on her head.

"I'm sorry Miss Charlotte. I overslept. I was so tired last night I forgot to set my alarm." I tried to think of something quick and easy to fix. "You make yourself comfortable, and I'll have something whipped up in a minute or two."

She mumbled plenty loud enough for me to hear. "I was afraid of that."

"Did you say something Miss Charlotte?"

"Oh, no, dear. You go ahead. I'll be fine in the living room by myself. It's a good thing I brought along that jar of fiber."

Please, help me keep my patience, Lord. And hurry!

I know God has better things to do than listen to me whine, but he must have heard my plea because I laid my hands on just the right ingredients for a nice meal.

I mixed chopped bell peppers, tomatoes, and cheese with eggs and poured the mixture into the hot skillet. I'd hoped an omelet would satisfy my hungry guest, but I overheated the skillet and the eggs were dry.

We'd almost finished pushing the food around our plates when the phone rang. "My goodness. Who would be calling this early?" I watched Miss Charlotte inspecting a scorched bit of omelet hanging on her fork.

"It could be business," I said.

"Well, you tell whoever it is we are still eating."

I grabbed the receiver. "Hello."

A cheery voice on the other end answered, "Hello, yourself. How's it going?" Honey chuckled, knowing full well how it was going.

"It's going," I said.

"She's right there isn't she?" Another giggle.

"You've got that right." I could feel Miss Charlotte's stare. I saw her out of the corner of my eye and sure enough she had stopped eating and had given me her full attention. Why did I let her get to me?

"Honey, I know I left a message for you to call, but we were just finishing up eating and I need to go. But I have something I want to talk to you and Ginger about. You won't believe who called me this morning!"

"The suspense is killing me. Eleven still okay?"

"Sure, see you then."

I went back and sat to finish the last bite or two of my omelet. "That was Honey. She and her cousin Ginger are coming over this morning. You remember Honey don't you?" Like you could ever forget Honey once you'd met her.

"Humph! Of course, I remember Honey." She dabbed her mouth with her napkin. "By the way, dear, what did you do with those pretty linen napkins and placemats I bought you for Christmas? I am sure Mitch prefers cloth."

I bit my tongue so hard I thought it would bleed. "I'll be sure and set them out. I need to clean up the kitchen and finish getting ready. Would you like to watch TV while I put on my makeup?"

"Oh, no! I'll just read. Too much television dulls the mind."

I heard my cell, so I dashed upstairs to answer it, managing to escape a lecture on how television had gone downhill ever since Carson retired.

CHAPTER FIFTEEN

I picked up the phone as it went to voicemail. Oh well, for now, Mitch was better off not knowing Daniel had called for my help.

I had the urge to crawl under the covers and pull them over my head. I knew it'd take every ounce of strength to make it through this day.

I straightened the room, put on makeup and went back downstairs to clean the kitchen. I'd finished loading the dishwasher when the doorbell rang. *The cavalry's arrived!*

I opened the door to my allies. Honey was dressed in her unique style as usual. She wore a pair of orange and white flowery capris paired with a white long-sleeved tee with holes along the outside length of her arms. She sported sandals decorated with an orange and white pom-pom. Pushed back in her hair were her favorite pair of black and white polka-dot sunglasses. And of course, her signature Merle Norman Romance Red lipstick. Only Honey could pull this off and look good doing it.

I pulled Honey in, exposing Ginger. The one thing Ginger had yet to give up was the way she dressed. She wore a short skirt, tight top and gladiator sandals laced almost up to her knees. I knew without a doubt, Ginger had a great desire to leave the old life behind, but her attire didn't reflect her ambitions yet. Honey was working on it, but didn't want to discourage her cousin. I had definitely learned; it was a travesty to judge people only by their appearance. But I knew Miss Charlotte would do just that.

Her jaw dropped so far I feared she'd lose her false teeth. Honey either didn't see her expression or ignored it. I expected it was the latter. She ran right over to Miss Charlotte and gave her a big hug!

"Hello, Lottie! It's so good to see you. It's been too long." Miss Charlotte pretended she didn't like the nickname, but had never asked Honey to stop.

Honey pulled Ginger closer. "This is my cousin, Ginger. She's staying with me for a while. I know you two will get along fine."

Miss Charlotte looked Ginger up and down. "Humph! Well, dear, that is certainly a unique ensemble. Doesn't it get a little breezy?" She gave a quick once over at Ginger's low cut blouse and short skirt.

I was mortified. I might think the same thing, but would never artic-ulate it. "Ginger, why don't you make yourself comfortable in Mitch's recliner?" She plopped in the recliner and promptly tugged at her skirt.

Honey broke the tension. "Skye, what have you got to tell us that's so important?" I saw her reach over and pat Miss Charlotte's hand. She was rewarded with a weak smile.

"Does anybody want anything to drink first?" Honey and Ginger shook their heads.

"I'll take some hot tea," Miss Charlotte said.

I grabbed a teabag and started to heat a cup of water in the microwave.

"Oh my, a teabag. This won't do. It's a good thing I brought some of my Earl Gray." She hurried into her room and we could hear her rummaging.

Honey shot me a look of sympathy while I searched for the kettle. "I'm dying to hear your news." I was happy to change the subject.

"Daniel Smith called early this morning. He's been arrested."

"What?" Honey said.

"Why?" Ginger wanted to know.

"They arrested him for Joan's murder."

Honey and Ginger jumped up and slapped palms. "Yes! That means

Ginger won't go to jail after all." Honey did a little happy dance but stopped mid toe kick. "Oh, I guess that's not good for Daniel, though. Did he tell you why they thought he did it?"

She sat beside a stunned Miss Charlotte who had come back in clutching her box of Earl Grey. We explained to her what had taken place in the past few days. I'm ashamed to say, I thought this served her right for inviting herself to stay with us.

"Lottie, don't you worry. Ginger didn't kill nobody. We think she was framed," Honey assured her.

It was the first time I'd ever seen Miss Charlotte speechless. "I think I'll go in the other room and let you girls catch up.

When she'd gone, Honey turned to me. "Well, spill it. On what grounds did they arrest him?"

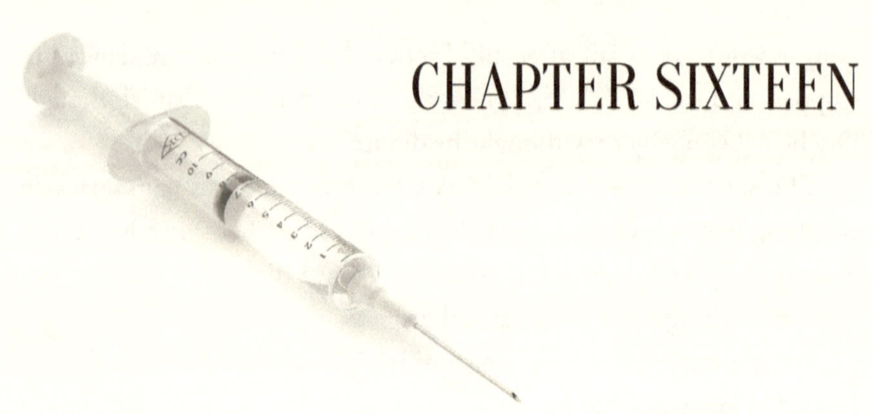

CHAPTER SIXTEEN

"That's just it. Daniel didn't get a chance to tell me. He wants to meet this afternoon when he gets out on arraignment. I told him I'd ask y'all first."

Honey watched me fill the kettle at the tap. "Why does he want to meet with us?"

"He thinks we can help him." I turned toward Ginger. "He said they kept asking him questions about your past relationship. They're determined to connect you to the crime. I don't see how they can with what little circumstantial evidence they have, but they're trying awful hard. He thinks if we can help find the killer both of y'all would be exonerated."

Honey's blonde curls danced as she shook her head. "How do we know he isn't the killer? He might be using us." She hopped up. "I've got to have a cup of coffee. Anybody else?"

"Help yourself, there's a pot already made." I checked the level in the carafe, and took the creamer out of the fridge.

Ginger voiced her concerns about getting involved with Daniel.

"I admit he's a liar and a womanizer, but that doesn't necessarily make him a murderer. We could meet him to find out what's going on," I said.

Honey poured three cups of coffee while I poured hot water over Miss Charlotte's tea, hoping I'd made it correctly.

"I guess it wouldn't hurt," Honey said. "You don't have to go along, Gin, you could stay here with Lottie."

Lottie, er, Miss Charlotte, accepted her cup of tea without complaint and I returned to the kitchen table.

Ginger said in a hushed tone. "Don't leave me here with her. I'll listen to what he has to say. Y'all gave me a second chance; I guess he deserves one too."

Ginger's mention of second chances took me back in time. I'll never forget when I threw a wild ball to my friend Pam, accidentally breaking a window in Daddy's prized 1965 Chevy Impala Super Sport. I nearly made myself sick worrying how he'd react. It didn't help when Mother kept telling me to "wait until your father gets home."

I tried to prolong the inevitable by hiding in my room. It didn't work. I heard Daddy's booming voice, "Skye, get down here right now." I walked downstairs in slow motion, head hung low, sniffling and wiping tears. I expected punishment for playing too close to his prized possession. I knew I deserved to be punished when I'd been warned numerous times not to throw ball in the front yard. My disobedience resulted in hurting Daddy. But punishment was not what I received. He gestured toward our couch. Daddy sat beside me. "Skye, we've asked you not to play ball out front. You see what can happen when you take matters in your own hands."

"I'm sorry, Daddy." I melted into his arms, sobbing and getting slobber all over his suit coat.

"I know you are. And I also know that it was an accident. And I can see you are sorry, so I forgive you. We all deserve a second chance."

I couldn't believe my ears. He wasn't going to punish me. I had really dodged the bullet. He went on to say it was that way with our Heavenly Father. He forgives us over and over. Each time we're forgiven we have a second chance to make it right. I didn't understand the comparison at the time, but as I got older it made sense. I wished I had a forgiving spirit like my daddy many times. I assured Daddy I'd never play ball close to the car again. And I didn't!

My trip down memory lane was abruptly interrupted. Honey shook my arm. "Skye! Where were you?"

"Oh, I was picking cotton."

Honey nodded. "I think the vote to meet Daniel is a unanimous yes."

"Okay, that settles it. Let's keep busy until he calls. This Saturday is too beautiful to waste. How about going to the Swan House for lunch?"

"I know you can get a decent meal there. George and I ate there several times over the years," Miss Charlotte said from the doorway.

"It's one of our favorites," Honey told her.

"Would you like to come along?" I decided to be the bigger person, doubting she'd want to be seen with us anyway. But she surprised me when she nodded.

"Well, I guess that would be all right. I'll need to freshen up and change my clothes if we're going out."

Freshen up? We'd only been up a few hours. "Okay, you go ahead Miss Charlotte and we'll wait for you to get ready."

While we waited for Miss Charlotte, we chatted about the beautiful house on Candler and the work ahead of us. I chomped at the bit to start the process. I had a file full of ideas in my mind. Miss Charlotte quickly returned.

"I'm ready!" She straightened her hat.

If she were going to meet the Queen maybe. Coordinated with the hat, she wore a simple black dress that fell right below the knees. She had on patent leather black pumps, a pearl necklace, hat and white gloves. She looked like she'd stepped right out of an outdated Good Housekeeping magazine.

Honey didn't skip a beat. "Lottie, you sure clean up good."

"If that means you think I look nice, I accept your compliment." With a twinkle in her eye, she picked a piece of lint off her dress and smoothed it down.

"You do look nice. That dress looks like something my grandmother would wear." Ginger said with a fondness I hadn't heard in her voice before.

Charlotte turned her focus on Ginger and I braced myself. "Is that what you're wearing, dear?" Her scrunched-up face reminded me of a wrinkled prune. I couldn't wait to hear Ginger's reply.

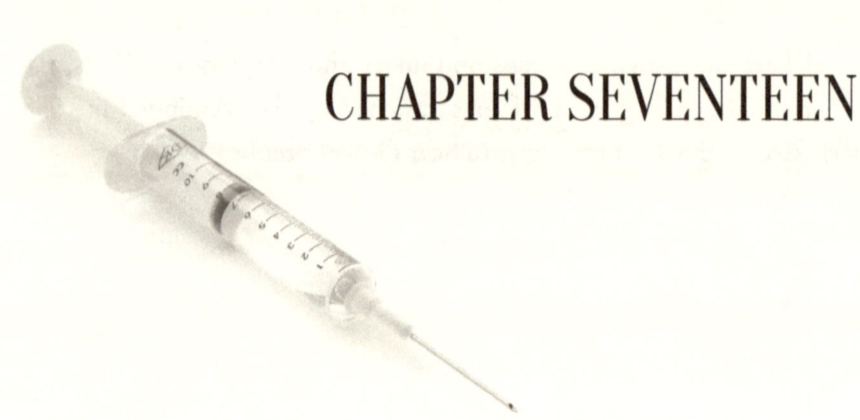

CHAPTER SEVENTEEN

She politely answered, "Yes, ma'am. It is. You see, I don't have a lot of money in order to buy lovely clothes like you're wearing."

I was dumbfounded when Charlotte ran a hand along Ginger's arm. "At least you've got the gams to carry off that short skirt."

Stunned, I finally found my voice and made a suggestion, "Let's get going before the lunch rush hits." I brought up the end of the line so I could lock the door. "I'd like to stop by the shop and pick up some swatches. Honey, can you remind me?"

"Sure. If Ginger reminds me to remind you." This brought a chorus of giggles except from Miss Charlotte. Honey laced arms with her. "Lottie, you have to admit that was pretty funny."

She shot Honey a smile. "It was a little humorous."

"All righty then. Let's hit the road, Jack!" Honey opened the front passenger door for Miss Charlotte. We piled into my Highlander and headed to the Swan House.

Saturday traffic on Peachtree Street was tolerable. It didn't take long to arrive. I knew for a fact Ginger had never been here. My old insecurities raised their ugly heads. Seeing the elegant surroundings of the tearoom triggered memories of another day in a similarly elegant restaurant. An angry wasp and a low cut blouse don't make for a peaceful meal. I glanced at Ginger to see if she was thinking the same, but so far she didn't seem worried.

A pretty blonde hostess stood sentinel by the front desk. "Hi. May I help you?"

"Yes. We need a table for four please," I said.

Honey piped up, "Could we sit on the terrace?"

I didn't want to put up a fuss, so we followed the girl outside like ducklings following their mother. She seated us and took our drink orders. "Cindi will be serving you today. She'll be with you shortly." She smiled and retreated inside.

The patio area was gorgeous. Forest green ivy covered the enclosed rock walls. Bright pink tablecloths were topped off with a vase of fragrant pink and yellow roses. Patrons filled the tables on the terrace.

Ginger's eyes grew wide. "Wow, this is even swankier than that restaurant where the yellow jacket attacked me. Hanging around y'all has definitely moved me up a notch on the social ladder."

I thought I saw Miss Charlotte roll her eyes and so I tried to engage her in conversation. "Miss Charlotte, what looks good to you?"

"Humph. Give me time. You can't rush an important decision."

Feeling deflated, I clammed up and went back to studying my menu.

Honey came to the rescue, bless her heart. "Well, I'm going to have their signature chicken salad. Their frozen fruit salad is famous, you know. How about you Gin?"

"There's so much to choose from. It all kinda' sounds fancy to me. Don't they have collards and cornbread like Mary Mac's?" She licked her lips.

"'Fraid not cousin. But I don't think you'll be disappointed with whatever you select."

"I'm betting they don't have squirrel soup like Mama used to make, but maybe they'll have good ole' vegetable beef. Got to have my meat. Okay, I'll take the soup and sandwich."

I looked over at Miss Charlotte in time to see the color drain from her face. I have to admit, she handled it like a trooper, though. She never missed a beat, "Well, I'll have the Salad Sampler." She gingerly placed her napkin in her lap and crossed her hands on top. No elbows on the table for her.

I settled for the Caribbean Chicken Salad. After Cindi took our orders we chatted and sipped tea until our food arrived.

My shoulders had finally relaxed past my ears, and I was enjoying the food and conversation. However, I'd let my guard down too soon. I froze when I spotted a visitor resting on the table.

Honey spotted it next. "Oh, look at the tree frog." About that time, it hopped right onto Ginger's spoon. Startled, she jumped to push away and her hand struck the other end of the spoon sending the frog airborne. What happened next could only be labeled a freaky ironic accident.

The little frog, with no control of the situation, landed down the front of Miss Charlotte's dress right between her bosom. I'm sure her scream could be heard by people visiting the Atlanta History Museum next door. I didn't know someone Miss Charlotte's age could jump up so fast. She was on her feet in a flash.

Ginger jumped up at the same time, knocking her tea over, spilling it over the table and onto Miss Charlotte's skirt. She grabbed her napkin and swiped at the front of Miss Charlotte's dress. "I'm sorry. I didn't mean to, Lottie."

Miss Charlotte pushed her hand away. "That is *Miss* Charlotte to you."

Honey ran over and tried to gracefully extract the frog from Miss Charlotte's dress, only making my mother-in-law angrier. Finally, she reached down and pulled the little bugger out. When she held the frog up everyone clapped.

"Come on, Miss Charlotte. We're not far from home. Let's go change your dress." We hurriedly gathered our things while I paid the bill, and left a generous tip because of the mess we'd made.

As we piled into the car my cell rang. "Hello."

"Skye," this is Daniel, "I'm out now. Can y'all meet me? Just name the place and time." I heard the desperation in his voice and imagined sweat trickling down his brow.

"Who is it?" Honey asked from the back seat.

"It's Daniel," I told them. *What now, Lord?*

CHAPTER EIGHTEEN

I told him to meet us at the shop in an hour, figuring that'd give us enough time to swing by the house and let Miss Charlotte change her frog-soiled clothes.

I gave him the address wondering how this was all going to play out. I hoped we weren't getting in over our heads. *We're just going to listen to what he has to say. That's all.* Famous last words.

Honey helped Miss Charlotte in while I opened the front door. Ginger waited in the car. I think she was feeling terrible about her part in ruining our lunch. It wasn't her fault this time, but I didn't have the time to worry about her feelings and Miss Charlotte's dress at the same time.

Honey and I chatted about Daniel's situation while Miss Charlotte changed. She came in the living room wearing a fresh black dress. "My other one will have to be dry cleaned dear."

"Of course, Miss Charlotte."

"Nice frock," Honey said.

The dress looked like all the others she wore. Lottie smiled and smoothed imaginary wrinkles.

I stood. "You ready to go?"

"I think I've had enough of your excitement for one day. A nap will do me good." She yawned. "I don't know how long it'll take me to get over the humiliation I was subjected to this afternoon. Maybe I'll call Mitch before I lie down."

If that was meant as a jab, she hit her target. I wasn't sure how Mitch would take the news about his mother and the flying frog. But I couldn't worry about that now. We needed to get on the road.

I made sure Mother Charlotte was comfortable before Honey and I made our escape . . . I mean getaway . . . no that's not right either. Oh, well, you know what I mean.

When we returned to my car, we discovered Ginger sound asleep in the back seat. Her head was flung back and lolled to one side. Drool had run down her chin. She woke when we shut the doors.

Honey pointed toward her mouth and handed her a tissue.

"I didn't realize how sleepy I was. Isn't Miss Charlotte coming with us?"

"No, she's resting from her ordeal." I cranked my Highlander and backed out of the driveway, not knowing what awaited us.

"I'm sorry I ruined lunch." Ginger scooted up between us. "I don't think she likes me very much."

I felt her pain. "It wasn't your fault. And I don't think she likes anyone very much. That is except Mitch. And possibly Honey. I tell myself not to take it personally, but it's hard. I wish I knew how to win her good graces."

"Well, when you find out, be sure and let me know." Ginger scooted back and refastened her seatbelt.

Daniel was sitting on an outside bench when we got there, petting a stray dog I'd seen in the neighborhood before. "Hey, I've been waiting. I thought you might have changed your mind and not come after all." He looked at Ginger, but spoke to the group. "I'm sorry to get you involved, but I'm a desperate man. I did *not* kill my wife! And I don't believe Ginger was there either. I think we were framed and somebody planned it to look like Ginger and I were in on the murder together."

Ginger avoided eye contact with Daniel and leaned over and ruffled the mutt's fur. "This little fellow wants something to eat." The little dog wore no collar, and his hair was matted. He definitely needed some attention.

"What a cutie pie," Honey said. "Skye, you've talked about getting a dog." She reached and picked him up. He rewarded her with a lick to the face. *Yuck!* "We have some snacks in the break room. Mind if I feed him?"

"We should at least get him off the street." I looked at him skeptically. "That's all I need. A dog *and* Miss Charlotte to take care of. I have to admit, he is cute, though."

Honey placed him back on the ground and he ran straight to me, placed his front paws on my leg and stared up at me. I reached down and petted him. "Good, boy. Want to come home with me?" I looked up to see Honey and Ginger grinning. "All right. I'll think about it.

I unlocked the door and turned to Daniel. "You come in as well and explain why Detective Haynes thinks you killed Joan." I led the way to my office while Honey took the dog on a snack finding mission. We moved stacks of materials from the chairs so we could sit.

"This is complicated," Daniel began, "but I'll try my best to break it down in layman terms." His right leg jiggled. He placed a firm hand on his knee, but his leg kept right on moving. "Let me give you a little background on myself first."

"I'm currently working in the field of Gerontology research. I love what I do." He looked our way daring us to dispute him. "Now, let's get the elephant out of the room. I know I wasn't a good husband."

Ginger murmured, "You've got that right."

Honey came in, but still he gave Ginger his undivided attention. "I'm sorry I lied to you. I've done my share of philandering and know I made Joan's life miserable." Ginger nodded, still not making eye contact. "And I admit, I was selfish and a jerk." He paused for a minute. "But I'm not a murderer."

The tension in the room could be sliced with a knife, so when my phone rang, I jumped, dumping a stack of papers off my lap.

CHAPTER NINETEEN

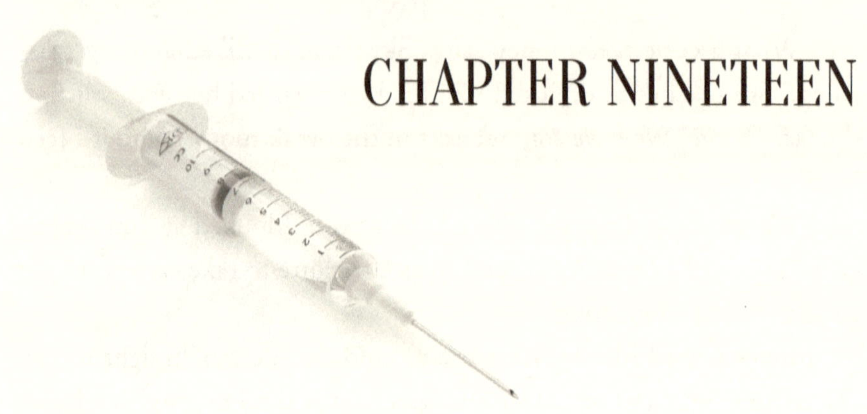

I checked the caller ID. *Mitch!* This was the second time he'd phoned. Had Miss Charlotte already tattled on me? I knew I'd have to tell him about Daniel sooner than later, but I let the call go. A twinge of guilt pricked me, but I didn't want to interrupt Daniel's story.

"I sent the call to voice mail, go ahead," I said. All attention returned to Daniel. I held my breath as he proceeded.

"Like I said, I love my patients. More and more were coming to me with early stage dementia. I don't know how many families I watched travel with their loved one through the stages of Alzheimer's disease."

His face tightened and his eyes misted. He continued, "It's an ugly, ugly illness and as you know there is no cure. I couldn't stand to see the suffering any longer. I retired as a practicing physician and went into research. I'd read there were some promising experiments in the near future. I wanted to be part of finding a cure for Alzheimer's.

Honey voiced my exact sentiments. "This is all well and good, Daniel, but what has it got to do with Joan's murder?"

"Yeah," Ginger agreed.

He ran his long fingers through his slicked back hair. I'm sure he'd used pomade and I wondered if they were greasy now. It's amazing how our mind follows rabbit trails while someone is talking. He leaned forward and placed his forearms on his knees demanding our attention.

"I know it's a long story and all of this doesn't seem relevant, but if you'll be patient you'll see how it all ties together. I was hired at a lab specializing in gerontology – specifically Alzheimer's research. I was ecstatic! They offered me research using organophosphates." We looked at him with blank expressions.

"Let me explain. Organophosphates is an ingredient found in pesticides. The reason is complicated, but all you need to know is my lab is researching ways to use them in the treatment of Alzheimers. Back in the 1990's it was used in minute amounts to treat the disease. But there weren't enough studies so they took if off the market for use in patients with dementia. The promising news is we have started testing organophosphates for this use again."

I looked at the time. I didn't want to leave Miss Charlotte alone too long. "Daniel, could you get to the point?"

"I'm almost there. I knew the police were suspicious of Joan's death, but I didn't know why, except they always start with close relatives and friends first. But when they arrested me, I found out the coroner found a needle prick in her arm. They tested her blood for poisoning and it came back with high levels of organophosphates. With the ready availability of the substance and needles at my disposal they pinned it on me.

"Then they brought up my past relationship with Ginger and the recent arguments she had with Joan." He shook his head. He leaned back in his chair, and a dark cloud seemed to engulf him. I had to admit, it didn't look good for him. And with his arrest, now the heat was likely on Ginger as well.

"Wow, Daniel. Your goose is cooked," Honey said. She laid a hand on Ginger's shoulder. "We'll figure this out, kiddo."

I asked the obvious question. "Did you kill her, Daniel?"

"Like I said, Skye, we didn't get along that great, but I had no reason to kill her. Organophosphates are readily available to anyone. People use pesticides in their home, gardeners use it on lawns and plants – don't you see it could have been anybody?"

Ginger paced back and forth. She stopped in front of Daniel. "Why would a gardener want to kill Joan?"

"In a way, a lot of people might have wanted her dead. She had a mean streak. Partly my fault for leaving her alone while I was at the hospital long hours. And my wandering. So the fact is, I really don't know who might have killed her. That's why I want y'all to help me."

I considered what I knew of Joan's relationships. "I know for a fact she wasn't well liked at the club." I looked at Daniel. "Sorry, but she had a tendency to look down her nose at people. And I've seen her on more than one occasion ridicule the help."

"I understand," he said. "We all have our faults and that was definitely one of Joan's. I really believe a lot of that came from low self-esteem." He had the decency to look contrite. "I'm sure my little escapades didn't help. I'd told her many times I'd give her a divorce so she could move on with her life, but she didn't want to go that route so we made the best of it. Anyway, she was miserable and took it out on everyone else." He bit his lower lip. "Lately, I've been on the straight and narrow. I was trying to do right by her."

I was beginning to feel sorry for him, and now that Ginger was involved, we had no choice. "We'll talk about how we can help and let you know our decision. In the meantime, could you come up with anyone you know of who might have had a motive to kill her?"

"Sure. I really appreciate your help. I want to stay out of jail and continue my research. I really do want to make it up to society and do some good for the world."

CHAPTER TWENTY

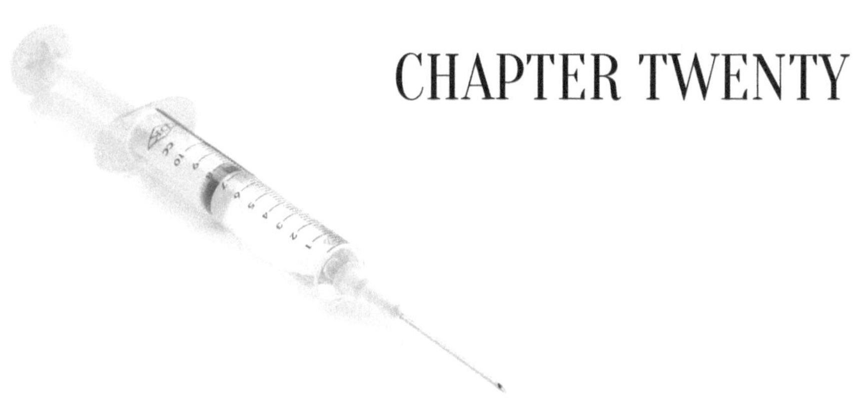

aniel left and I gathered materials I needed to take home with me. I didn't want to leave Miss Charlotte alone too long. I'd promised Mitch I'd keep an eye on her, and I'd fallen down on the job.

Ginger waited outside with the dog. "Well, are you going to take him?"

"I'd almost forgotten." The little dog stood wagging his tail, looking at me with his big brown eyes. "Sure, I'll take him, but I'll have to advertise to see if anyone's lost a dog. He looks like somebody's pet." What would Mitch think? *Oh, well, if he can bring home Miss Charlotte without letting me know, I could bring home a dog.* But if I knew Mitch, a sucker for abandoned animals, he'd welcome him into the family.

I locked up, and we planned to meet again tomorrow after church to make our decision. The dog, in the front seat with me, stood with his paws on the window. I hoped he was housebroken. If not, I was in for some work. "Hey, buddy, whatcha see out there? That's it! I'll name you Buddy." *That was easy.* The smell of dirt emanated from Buddy. I'd have to give him a bath tonight if he was going to stay inside.

Grabbing Buddy, I hurried in the house. "Miss Charlotte, I'm home," I called out, but all I could hear was the TV blaring. I released Buddy on the floor and he took off, sniffing the furniture, and we found Miss Charlotte asleep in Mitch's recliner. *Well, so much for not watching television.* I shook her shoulder, but she continued to snore. I leaned down to call her name when the smell of alcohol hit me square in the face. Sitting on the side table was a small decorative flask.

"Miss Charlotte!" That got her attention. Her eyes popped open and she jumped out of the chair.

I picked up the flask. "What's this?"

"That's a little red wine I have every evening for medicinal purposes only." It must have worked, because she moved better than I'd seen in a long time.

"No need to tell Mitch about this." She put her finger to her lips. "This will be our little secret." She plopped right back into the chair.

Buddy jumped into Miss Charlotte's lap, circled, and laid beside her. She scooted over, "What in the world is this mutt doing? He's got paw-prints on my dress."

I ran over and scooped Buddy off Miss Charlotte. "I'm sorry. This is Buddy, a stray I brought home. Don't worry, I'm going to advertise and see if anyone's lost a pet, but in the meantime, he stays here."

"Humph!" One of Miss Charlotte's favorite sayings. "What do you want with a dog?"

I ignored her rant. I looked at the clock and knew I'd have to hurry to clean Buddy and have supper ready. Miss Charlotte went into her room while I was busy. I guess she didn't want Buddy's company.

Buddy went to the front door and started whining. "You need to go out, boy?" He performed a little tap dance. I opened the door and he flew out. I feared he'd run off and I'd lose him, but he did his business and returned. It was a relief to know he was house trained.

I was putting supper on the table when Mitch arrived. He made a beeline for me and gave me a bear hug. "Yum, you smell good. Kind of like steak?"

I laughed a belly laugh for the first time in days. "It's my new eau de parfum. I'm glad you approve."

Buddy yipped, trying to get our attention. Mitch scratched him behind the ears. "Well, where did you come from little bit?" He looked up at me, "Skye, did you have something to do with this?"

I lifted my hands in surrender. "Guilty as charged. He's been hanging around the shop. I couldn't leave him alone. I gave him a bath and he's already lookin' better. His name's Buddy."

"He's a cute bugger." Mitch picked him up and scratched Buddy's belly.

"I'll check the lost and found websites for the area and call the shelter tomorrow."

"The vet can scan him for a chip," Mitch reminded me. "Maybe we can keep him if no one claims him."

"Thank you." I gave him a smack on the lips. "Supper is about ready. As soon as you freshen up it'll be on the table."

Supper went smoothly and Miss Charlotte asked for seconds. I served country-fried corn, New York Strip steaks, and a baked potato. If her appetite was any clue, she enjoyed my efforts.

The rest of the evening was quiet. Miss Charlotte retired early to read, Mitch snored in his recliner and I watched a little of my favorite show, an English sitcom on PBS called "Keeping up Appearances." My eyes kept closing and popping open. My bed called, and just as I mustered up the energy to get there, the landline rang. I glanced at the time – ten p.m. Who would be calling this late?

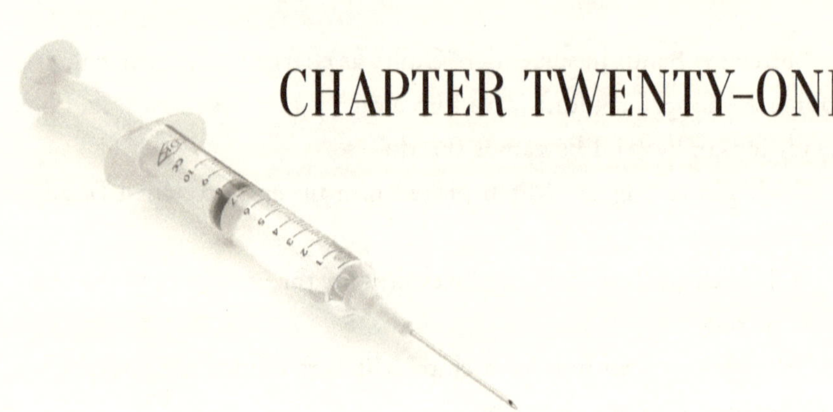

CHAPTER TWENTY-ONE

"Hey, Skye, did I wake you?"

"No. I had to wake up to answer the phone." Honey's laughter lifted my spirit.

"I couldn't wait to tell you about my date with Robert." Her unadulterated enthusiasm reminded me of my teenage years and chatting with girlfriends about our dates. I hadn't seen her this happy since Frank had died. After losing two husbands, I wasn't sure she'd want to date again. All that changed when she met Robert Montaine, the detective on Sylvia Landmark's case.

"You didn't get engaged did you?" It'd only been a few months since they'd started dating.

A squeal assaulted my ear, "No, but we've decided to be in a committed relationship."

I couldn't help poking fun. "Does that mean y'all will be committed to the home for the bewildered?"

"Funny! I think I'm in love, Skye." I pictured her, hand over heart, swaying back and forth.

"I'm glad for you, Honey. Robert seems like a great guy." I'd grown to like the hunky detective. "Speaking of Robert, did y'all discuss the case at all?"

"I told him about Daniel wanting our help. Of course, he warned me about getting involved, but he said he knew he was wasting his breath.

He wouldn't divulge anything new. I think we'd better not count on him for information."

While we chatted I let Buddy outside one last time for the evening. "You're probably right. He doesn't want to jeopardize his job." I told her about cleaning up Buddy and finding Miss Charlotte with her *medicinal* wine. We laughed at her ingenuity. Tomorrow was Sunday so we planned to meet at church and go to lunch afterwards.

"I'm glad Mitch is okay with having a dog. Oh, and hey, Robert's going to meet us at church. I'm so excited. He'll get to meet some Jesus loving, on-fire-for-God people."

We said good-night and I dragged myself upstairs. I slipped on my pajamas and literally fell into bed. I hadn't realized how tired I was. Sleep came quickly, but it was filled with dreams.

Joan held a red high heel as she chased Ginger through the lobby of the clubhouse. In the next scene Joan chased Daniel waving the red shoe yelling, "Cheater!" Then, Daniel and Ginger stood over Joan's dead body with Detective Haynes in the background holding handcuffs.

Somebody was shaking me. My eyes popped open.

"Honey, you all right?" Mitch leaned over me. "You were talking in your sleep."

"What did I say?" I hoped it wasn't embarrassing.

"You said, "Cheater!" I hope you weren't dreaming of me." Mitch laughed.

"No. I dreamed about Daniel and Joan." I'd told Mitch about Daniel asking for our help. Like Robert, he thought we should stay out of it. Especially since Ginger had been questioned. I informed him that was precisely why we needed to get involved.

I snuggled against Mitch. He placed his arm around me. The warmth of his body soothed my unquiet spirit, and I slept peacefully the rest of the night.

Morning came way too soon. I pried open my eyes and cat walked down the stairs so as not to wake Miss Charlotte and let Buddy out. As we came back in, she emerged from her room fully dressed.

"Did you oversleep, dear?" Miss Charlotte smoothed away invisible wrinkles on her dress – obviously a habit. "It's seven already and you haven't even started breakfast."

I bit my tongue. It was going to be mutilated before Miss Charlotte went home. "We have plenty of time before church. I think you'll like the new one we attend. Everyone is so friendly."

"That's nice. They don't do any of that snake handling do they?"

Where in the world did that come from? I'd heard about snake handling churches and had seen a documentary on one that used to be in Kingston, Georgia, but I'd never attended one. "No, ma'am."

The rest of the morning flew and before I knew it, it was time to leave for Holy Ground Community Church. Miss Charlotte had donned heels, gloves, pearls and a hat. I swanny, she looked like she'd stepped out of a 1950's Sears catalog.

We squeezed together on one pew, landing me between Ginger and Miss Charlotte. I looked from one to the other. The differences proved God's children come in all different packages. Ginger, who'd attended regularly since she'd been staying with Honey, had been embraced with open arms – unique wardrobe and all. The welcome would be no less enthusiastic for Miss Charlotte.

<hr>

We decided on Mary Mac's for lunch. Even though it was right smack dab in downtown Atlanta, I hoped the down home meals like Momma used to make would please Miss Charlotte.

It wasn't unusual to meet famous people at Mary Mac's. Not long ago we'd seen Jimmy and Roselyn Carter. I was a little taken aback though when Miss Charlotte said, "I declare! There's Mary Kay Andrews." Before I could blink, Miss Charlotte had made her way to a table filled with people. She stopped by an attractive middle-aged woman. I quickly followed her.

"Why, you're May Kay Andrews aren't you?" she said in the voice of an Atlanta Braves umpire. Every head in the dining room turned.

Lord, please let her be Mary Kay Andrews.

The woman wiped her mouth with a cloth napkin and placed it in her lap. "Yes, ma'am, I am. And who are you?"

"Why, I'm your biggest fan, Charlotte Oglethorpe Southerland!"

I learned Mary Kay was a well-known writer from the Atlanta area. She was so gracious to Miss Charlotte and even autographed a menu for her. When we returned to our table she couldn't quit talking about her favorite author.

We ordered and Miss Charlotte continued her story about how Mary Kay's real name is Kathy Trocheck and she had written a series of cozy mysteries. Seeing her so animated and excited made her seem almost amenable. Could there be a real person inside the austere façade she wore most of the time? I vowed to try and find the real Charlotte.

We were still eating when my phone rang. "This is Daniel. I hope I didn't interrupt your Sunday, but I couldn't wait any longer. I've thought of some more things we need to consider about Joan's death."

CHAPTER TWENTY-TWO

I thought quickly and excused myself from the table. "I can't talk now, but why don't you meet us at the shop in a couple of hours?"

"Okay. I'll see you then."

Honey, inquisitive as ever, asked who it was. Wanting to cut the conversation short, I told her it was a client.

Mitch announced he needed to work for a little while that afternoon, which wasn't unusual in our line of work. "You don't mind entertaining, Mother, do you?" He offered a weak smile.

"I need to work as well, but we'd be glad to have you join us, Miss Charlotte."

"I think I'll take a nap this afternoon."

I didn't realize I'd been holding my breath, until I released it. Charlotte covered her mouth and yawned. Was she trying to get out of going? It didn't matter, really, I was relieved we wouldn't have to take Miss Charlotte to meet with a suspected killer.

We made arrangements to meet at the office, and Miss Charlotte chatted about Mary Kay on the way back to the condo. The conversation was pleasant until it took an unexpected turn. "Dear, what are you planning on cooking for supper tonight? All this eating out is messing with my plumbing."

"I haven't decided yet, but don't you worry I'll come up with something. We don't want your pipes to clog." I bit back a grin.

"You are so right. I see you're beginning to understand the importance of a home-cooked meal."

My zinger had gone right over her head. Oh, well, it was a good thing. I didn't want her upset, because she'd turn around and upset Mitch. When I arrived home, Buddy had left a little puddle in the kitchen floor. Poor baby. That was the problem with having indoor pets.

"Oh, my! Look what that dog has done. And right in the kitchen. I hope you plan on disinfecting with Clorox after you clean that up," Miss Charlotte said. She had to side-step the offensive puddle to get to her bedroom. I heard her muttering from her room.

I let Buddy out while I cleaned. He probably didn't need to go now, but I didn't want to take any chances.

Upstairs, I changed into khakis paired with a red tee, and I slipped on a pair of sandals. When I went back downstairs I heard snoring drifting from the bedroom. Miss Charlotte was already asleep. I left a note on the counter to make herself at home, not that she wouldn't anyway, and I'd be back in time to cook supper. I told Buddy goodbye and he rolled over for a quick belly scratch before I headed out the door.

Honey's red Crossfire stood outside the shop. I grabbed my keys and purse and hurried in.

"Get Lottie all settled?" Honey gave me a wry smile. She loved to give me a hard time and she knew Miss Charlotte could fluff my dander in short order.

"Very funny. You wouldn't be so forgiving if she was your mother-in-law. Come to think of it you didn't even have to deal with mother-in-laws." Her husbands had been so much older than her that their mothers were gone before they married Honey. I knew it was a cheap shot, but my nerves were raw from dealing with Mitch's mother.

Daniel came in the front door as we were gathering swatches for the Candler house.

"Good afternoon, ladies."

Honey got right to business. "You told Skye you thought of something else?"

I glanced at his ankle and noticed the bulge under his pant leg. I reminded myself we were doing this for Ginger as much as we were for Daniel.

"The week before she died, she bragged about getting the new gardener at the club fired."

"Do you know his name?"

"Why? What happened?" Honey demanded.

"Not sure. He was Mike something-or-other. I don't remember her mentioning a last name."

"Don't worry, we can find out," Honey said. "It's a good place to start. Don't y'all think?"

We nodded, and agreed we needed to question the suspects before it got too late.

"One more thing," Honey stopped Daniel before he left. "My boyfriend asked if you'd retained a lawyer yet."

Daniel's face fell. "I've been making inquiries, but no one's returning my calls. I have plenty of money, but no one seems interested in defending me."

Ginger spoke up. "How many of their wives did you hit on?"

He shook his head. "You're right, I'm being black balled. My old ways are really haunting me now."

We watched him leave, more determined than ever we'd find out who really killed Joan.

CHAPTER TWENTY-THREE

By the time Daniel left, it was already late afternoon. I'd have to hurry to get home in time to cook Miss Charlotte something for supper.

After another hour of work, we called it quits for the day. "How about y'all come over for supper? You can help entertain Miss Charlotte."

"I don't know Skye. Lottie might not want company." Honey smiled. I knew she was giving me a hard time.

"I'm fixing fried chicken, mashed potatoes with gravy and a green vegetable. And, I think I'll pick up a German Chocolate cake from the Farmer's Market." I knew Honey couldn't resist my fried chicken. The cake sealed the deal.

"Well, I'm coming, whether Honey does or not," Ginger said. "I'm not about to miss a home cooked meal like Mama used to make." Ginger looked at Honey incredulously. "Count me in, Skye."

"Oh, good grief! Y'all can't take a little joke. Of course, I'll come. Not about to miss your fried chicken. No way Lottie can complain about your best dish." Honey licked her lips.

"I wouldn't bet on that. I think she does it for spite. I don't understand why she doesn't like me." I wasn't defeated, though. She may have won a battle or two, but I planned on winning the war.

"Let's go ahead and load this stuff into the Highlander and we'll be ready to go tomorrow." I heaved a sample board out of my way. "Why don't we plan on meeting at the club for lunch and we can talk to Mike?" It was a good way to kill two birds with one stone. Maybe it wouldn't look so obvious why we were really there.

"Sounds good to me. We can scoot on over to Candler after we eat," Honey said. "I've got another date with Robert tomorrow night for supper, so don't even think about making any kind of plans after four. I need to get home and do a makeover before he picks me up." She flipped her blonde hair over her shoulder, reminding me of Miss Piggy. Not that I'd ever tell her.

Ginger had already started loading the car, so Honey and I hurried and picked up the slack. They followed me in Honey's Crossfire – or rather they passed me. Honey transformed into a racecar driver whenever she sat behind the wheel of her sporty car. I stopped for the cake, so Honey and Ginger were already in the condo when I arrived home.

I opened the door, and Buddy ran to greet me. I reached and scratched behind his ears. Miss Charlotte, deep in conversation with Honey, leaned forward and hung onto every word she said. I longed for that kind of attention from her. Ginger sat in Mitch's recliner, looking a little reticent. After her remarks about Ginger's dress the other day, I don't think Ginger trusted Miss Charlotte. Although, Ginger wore a pair of skinny jeans today, an improvement over the short dress.

"Hello! Everybody make yourselves at home while I fry the chicken."

"Oh, my! Fried chicken? I'm not sure my stomach can handle fried food. Jennifer bakes mine." Jennifer being her assistant, maid and cook. I wished Jennifer was here right now. I mouthed the words 'I told you so,' to Honey.

Honey came to my defense. "Now, Lottie, true southerners have to have fried chicken every now and then. I bet you can tolerate it this once." Honey patted Miss Charlotte's hand.

Miss Charlotte looked at Honey like she held the wisdom of the world. "I guess you're right. It won't hurt this once."

I made a quick decision to run upstairs and lay down my purse before I used it as a weapon. I stopped right then and there and knelt by my bed. I asked for forgiveness and the strength to make it through the next couple of weeks. I prayed for guidance to help Daniel and Ginger. When I got off my knees I felt a new found peace. How long that would last I didn't know, but for now I had the courage to face Miss Charlotte.

I set about cooking and left the entertainment crew to their job. Mitch arrived as I finished up. I was so happy to see him and I knew his mother would be, too.

He came up behind me and nibbled my neck. He whispered in my ear, "How about wearing that pink teddy tonight?" I felt my cheeks warm. He grabbed my waist from behind. "Well, what do you say?"

CHAPTER TWENTY-FOUR

turned and playfully slapped Mitch on the chest and wiggled my eyebrows. "Well, you never know what might happen behind closed doors." I gave him a quick kiss. "Wash up, supper's ready. All I have to do is set the table."

"The chicken sure smells good." He pointed to a thick, crunchy chicken breast. "I'm starved." He reached over, broke off a piece of crispy skin and popped it in his mouth.

I didn't know how long Honey had been standing there, but was pretty sure she'd heard some, if not all, of our conversation. "All right, you two love birds. Let's get this show on the road. I'm hungry!" She grabbed the plate of chicken and headed toward the dining room. Ginger grabbed the mashed potatoes and followed.

Dinner proceeded without incident. Honey and Ginger helped clean up then we all headed to the living room. We talked for a while, until Honey announced she needed her beauty sleep. I expected her to bristle when Ginger told Honey if that was the case, they'd better turn in early.

Honey took it in stride and laughed with the rest of us. Miss Charlotte said she needed to retire early, too. Mitch offered me a wink and a devious smile. I couldn't help but return the smile.

I let Buddy out one last time, realizing I'd grown fond of him. I secretly hoped no one would answer my post. I told the girls good night and waited to see Miss Charlotte settled in her room.

I headed upstairs to put on my pink teddy. I never admitted to Honey how much it "cranked Mitch's tractor," her words not mine. Somehow, I had a feeling she already knew.

"Whoa! Come here sexy mama." Mitch patted the bed. With a twinkle in his eye he said, "pink becomes you."

It had been a while since we'd spent quality time together. I looked forward to . . .

Crash! I grabbed Mitch's arm, "Mitch, did you hear that?" He hopped out of bed and pulled on his pants while I threw on a robe.

He flipped on the light and flew down the stairs. I followed on his heels. I expected to see an intruder. I didn't expect to see Miss Charlotte sitting in the middle of the kitchen floor. "Well, don't stand there gaping! Help me up."

"Miss Charlotte, are you all right? What happened?" It wasn't funny, but seeing her sitting on the floor with her hair in pin curls, arms crossed, tickled my funny bone. I took an arm to help her up, but she pulled it away and grabbed Mitch's outstretched hand.

"I was getting a snack when that fool dog ran in front of me and tripped me up. Knocked me right off my feet." Mitch pulled her up and I slid a kitchen chair behind her. She plopped down. "I don't know why you want that nasty dog in the house." The statement was addressed to me.

By this time, I was close enough to smell the alcohol on her breath. I looked, and sure enough the flask had slid across the floor and landed under the edge of the counter. I stood behind her and made a drinking motion with my hand to alert Mitch. He nodded.

"Mother, have you been drinking?" I knew Mitch hated to broach the subject, but it needed to be done.

If looks could kill, I'd be dead. "Whatever gave you that idea?" I held my gaze. I would not be intimidated. Well, not this time anyway.

"I can smell your breath, mother."

"Mitch, my rheumatism has been acting up. I just need a little for medicinal purposes."

Yeah, and her *medicine* might be the reason she didn't see Buddy.

Speaking of Buddy, I hadn't heard a peep from him. Guess he went and hid from all the commotion.

"All right, Mother. If you're not hurt, let's get you back in the bed," Mitch offered.

"My back hurts. I'll probably need more medicine." She searched for her flask. I had no intention of telling her where it landed.

Mitch helped his mother stand. "Honey, why don't you go on back to bed and I'll be there in a minute after I see to Mother."

I was more than happy to escape. I wanted to stay up for Mitch, but I dozed off waiting for him to return.

"Skye," Mitch gently shook me, "are you awake?"

I rolled over and offered him a smile. "I am now."

"We need to talk." A frown indicated the seriousness of his concern. "I'm worried about Mother's drinking."

"Is it a real problem?" This was news to me. I couldn't picture Miss Prim and Proper ever abusing alcohol. Especially, since I'd heard her call it the devil's vice.

Mitch sat beside me. "I never told you, because I knew she wouldn't want me to. But, when I was in elementary school, and Daddy was working long hours, she drank to mask the pain of loneliness.

"I always wondered why she didn't come to any of my school events." He hesitated as if remembering. "I didn't know anything was wrong until Daddy said she had to go away to the hospital for a while." I could see the hurt little boy in the grown man. "It wasn't until I was a teenager that I fully understood what had happened. Daddy cut back his work hours and as far as I know she didn't drink after that."

I reached over and hugged him. "I'm sorry, Mitch. I didn't know."

"I know, babe. There were times I wanted to tell you, but didn't want to break her confidence. I didn't want you to think less of her than you already do."

Ouch! That hurt. Mitch was right. I wore a chip on my shoulder when it came to Miss Charlotte. I vowed somehow to change our relationship. For Mitch's sake – and mine.

"My concern is that with Daddy gone and her living alone, she's started drinking again."

CHAPTER TWENTY-FIVE

"**M**aybe she does experience a lot of pain. You might be able to convince her to go to the doctor and see if anything is really wrong. And I'll keep a closer watch on her. I'll encourage her to get out of the house and go with me and the girls."

He sat up a little straighter. "You'd do that?"

"Of course." I wasn't so sure of what I was getting myself into. How was I going to explain checking out suspects for a murder investigation?

"I really appreciate it, hon. How about we get some sleep." He turned over and laid down. So much for my pink teddy.

The alarm jolted me from a deep sleep. Mitch had already left for work, leaving me to sleep in. I heard Buddy whining downstairs. Time to go out.

I donned my robe and padded down the stairs. I stopped in my tracks and drew in a gasp! Miss Charlotte sat at the dining room table in her nightgown with her hair still in pin curls. Was the world coming to an end?

I opened the front door and Buddy flew out. "What's wrong Miss Charlotte? Are you hurting from your fall last night?" She looked at me, not even making the effort to throw a retort in my direction. I felt a twinge of empathy after Mitch's revelation last night. Then I remembered my promise to him.

"Look. Ginger, Honey and I are going to the club for lunch today. We'd love for you to join us." I left out the part about interviewing Mike. She'd find out soon enough.

She raised her head, and I thought I detected a smile. "Okay. You know, when George was alive we used to go the club all the time. After he passed, I didn't want to go by myself." I thought of how lonely she must be.

"Well, you go ahead and get dressed, and I'll fix us up some breakfast. How about French toast?" She nodded and retreated to her room. By the time I'd gotten ready and had her breakfast on the table, she appeared. If I didn't know better, I'd have thought she was going to a funeral.

"Oh, my! You're dressed up today." She wore a dark blue, shirtwaist dress with a lace collar. I wondered if she wore panty hose or used a garter belt? I voted garter belt.

"George and I always dressed for the occasion when we ate at the club." She had certainly *dressed* for the occasion.

After breakfast, I reluctantly called the paper and asked them to run an ad for Buddy's owner. Before heading to the club, I stopped by Stylish Décor to pick up supplies. I couldn't wait to get my hands on the Candler jewel.

Honey and Ginger were waiting for us. Ginger and Miss Charlotte exchanged wary looks. The leaping frog incident popped into my mind.

I explained that Miss Charlotte would be accompanying us today. *And the next few days.* We took the Highlander with Ginger and Honey sitting in the back and Miss Charlotte up front with me.

I glanced in the rearview mirror to see Honey putting on her lipstick. I had to admit, it looked great on Honey, but most everything did. She'd been begging me to try it – maybe I would someday. She insisted Mitch would love it.

She caught me staring. "Want to borrow some?" She shook it for good measure. "I bet Mitch would love it. You could put it on when you wear your pink teddy." Ginger and Honey guffawed. I looked over at Miss Charlotte. She didn't seem to think it was funny at all.

Miss Charlotte let out a long sigh before speaking her mind. "Do y'all really need to be discussing this?"

"Aw, come on Lottie," Honey said, "life is too short to be taken seriously. It's good for your health to laugh."

"Humph," was all Miss Charlotte had to say.

Miss Charlotte insisted she didn't want to eat outside on the terrace. Ginger agreed. We decided on a table by the window. Sunshine filtered onto our white tablecloth spreading shards of glowing light. The colorful fresh cut flowers smelled heavenly.

All of us chose different entrees. When the waitress left, we sat back and relaxed. "Now, isn't this nice Miss Charlotte?" I hoped to receive an affirmation for asking her along.

"I guess so," she said.

Well, don't get beside yourself with joy. Making this relationship work was going to be harder than I thought. But I wasn't giving up. This had now become a personal challenge. The gauntlet had been thrown.

"Hey, do you think Mike will even be here if he's been fired?" Honey twirled the cloth napkin in her hands. Was she nervous? No. Not Honey.

"I didn't think about that. I guess I've had a lot on my mind," I said. Rookie mistake.

"If he's not here, we'll just find out where he lives." Ginger was getting the hang of this detective stuff. Then again, it was her freedom on the line.

"Who in the world is this Mike you keep talking about?" Miss Charlotte asked. The time had come to explain what we'd gotten ourselves into.

Tammy, our waitress, delivered our meals, freshened our tea and left. This was the perfect time to tell Miss Charlotte the news.

"My, goodness! Skye, what have you gotten these girls into?" She shook her head like she couldn't believe I'd do such a thing.

I longed to come back with a smart retort, but decided that would be wrong. By the time Honey told the story, we'd finished eating. "Let's go see if we can find Mike," I said.

It was a beautiful day. The sky mimicked a brilliant blue canopy with not a cloud in sight. God had painted the trees and bushes various shades. I loved how the color green had so many brilliant variations.

"Miss Charlotte, why don't you sit here on the terrace while we attend to some business."

No sooner had the words left my mouth when I saw him across the lawn disappearing through some hedges. I jumped up, yelled and waved my arms. "Hey, Mike!"

CHAPTER TWENTY-SIX

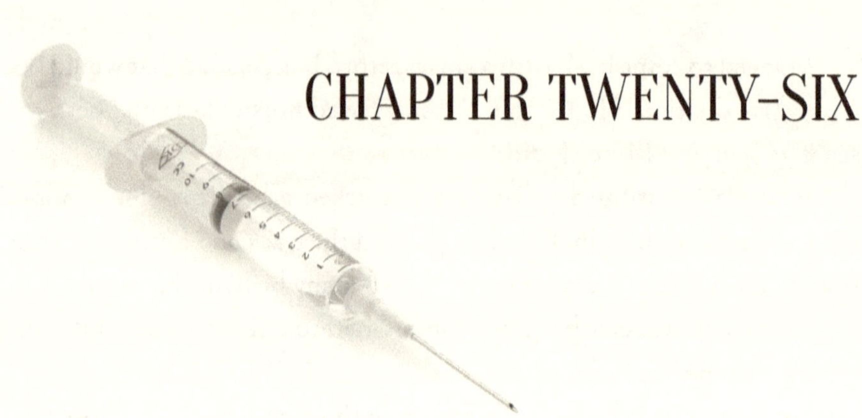

I ran across the lawn to catch up with him. Honey and Ginger were closing in. Sweat ran down my forehead and my clothes were disheveled, but Honey looked like she'd stepped off a magazine page with not one blonde hair out of place. I suppose if I wore a can of hair spray every day mine wouldn't be messed up, either. Honey loved to boast she alone could keep her hairspray company afloat.

"Why didn't you stop?" I struggled to regain my breath as I caught up to Mike.

"What do you want?" He was carrying bags of tools to a van.

"We want to ask you some questions about Joan Smith," I panted.

Mike placed his hands on his hips. "Why do you want to discuss Joan?"

"Is there a place we can talk in private?"

"I'm busy. I'm taking out my own equipment from the toolshed where my office is located – or was located." He gave us a cursory glance, all except Ginger, who had Mike's full attention.

"Okay. I suppose we could talk in my office," he said.

"Who's going to stay with Miss Charlotte?" I didn't want to leave her alone. Besides, I could tell Ginger might be an asset to this interview. "Why don't you go back, Honey?"

She agreed, and trekked back across the lawn to the terrace where Miss Charlotte waited.

I'd love to know what Honey did that made it so much easier for her to get along with Miss Charlotte. But I didn't have time for a lesson right now. I wanted to get on with this interview.

"Okay, lead the way."

Mike lead us to a large building filled with gardening tools. We followed him to the back where a small area had been designated for his office. A small desk and chair sat in the corner.

He started to sit in the only chair when he noticed Ginger leaning against a wall. "Oh! Where are my manners? Ginger, isn't it?" She nodded. "Would you like to sit here?"

Ginger batted her eyes, and her mouth turned into a cute little pucker. I expected her to pull out a paper fan any minute. She could have played Scarlet in the community theater production of "Gone with the Wind." *Oh, brother.* I rolled my eyes.

I looked at Ginger, but directed my comment to Mike. "Okay, if everybody's settled, I have some questions I'd like to ask you about Joan."

"Why?"

Think fast, Skye. I could use the fact he was smitten with Ginger for my benefit. "Ginger has been implicated in Joan's murder." Mike's eyes widened. I was curious how he'd react when I said the word, "murder" but he didn't seem fazed. Good actor? Or not guilty?

"We know she didn't do it, but the police aren't taking us seriously so we're doing some investigating of our own to help her."

"Well, if that's the case, fire away. Anything to help this little lady." It never ceased to amaze me how Honey and Ginger could turn a head quicker than butter melting on a hot biscuit.

I shot from the hip, "We heard she got you fired. Is that right?"

"Yeah, she did. Pure evil if you ask me." He placed one foot on a hay bale, grabbed a straw and stuck it in his mouth.

I couldn't help but wonder where that piece of hay had been. "What happened that she would want to get you fired?"

He shook the straw at me. "Well, it's like this. I was minding my own business, trimming the hedges around the tennis courts. All of a sudden she came over and told me to quit staring at her. I admit she was okay looking, but I sure wasn't staring. I needed my job and wasn't about to lose it by gawking at some middle-aged rich lady."

He said middle-aged like it was a dirty word.

"Then what happened?"

"By that time all the other ladies had stopped playing tennis and were watching us. She yelled and started acting all crazy, and she called me a liar. By this time, she had me riled up." He sat on the hay bale and pulled out a new straw. He pointed at a bale across from him, "Have a seat ma'am."

My feet ached, so I happily complied. "Did the others hear her call you a liar?" I longed to take off my shoes and rub my feet.

"No. With one of the other men mowing the grass they couldn't hear; they could just see."

Ginger piped up. "Her husband said you were fired because you hit her. Did you?"

CHAPTER TWENTY-SEVEN

ike's eyebrows shot up to his hairline and he came up right off that bale of hay. "Now look here. I might've made a lot of bad choices in my life, but I've never hit a woman. And I never plan on hitting one."

Ginger frowned. "Sorry, we're just asking because that's what we've been told."

For a guy who claimed to be nonviolent, he sure got riled in a hurry.

"If you didn't hit her how did the rumor get started?" I tried to find a smooth spot on the hay. The stray pieces went right through my clothes and stuck my bottom.

"After she called me a liar, I knew it was time for her to go back to her playmates. A bee landed on her shoulder and when I tried to shoo it off, I accidentally hit her." Mike paced back and forth, hands clasped behind his back. "She pushed me, yelling at me to keep my filthy hands off her. By that time, I was steaming. I told her to go back to her tennis game and walked off." I heard her yell, 'I'll have your job, you wait and see.'"

"That's quite a story, Mike." I questioned his truthfulness. It was her word against his and she wasn't here to defend herself. But the fact was, he lost his job because of her. Could he have been mad enough to kill her?

"Mike, do you have access to pesticides?"

"Of, course. Making sure the plants were healthy was part of my job. Why?"

"There's a possibility she was poisoned."

He stopped pacing, stood in front of me and looked down with eyes narrowed. "Are you suggesting I had something to do with her death?"

I scooted back on the hay bale. "Does anyone else have access to the pesticides?"

He thought a minute. "Now you mention it, the shed was broken into a few weeks ago. And yeah, several people on the staff have a key to this building. Any number of people can come in and out." He started gathering more items off the wall. "You also might want to take a look at her tennis partners. Word has it one of them was having an affair with her husband. None of them were really friends with her. They just needed a fourth person on the team."

"How did you know that?" Ginger asked.

He laughed, "People acted like I was invisible or couldn't hear them. Like people talking loud in a restaurant. I've heard a lot of stuff that would make your toes curl. If I wasn't such a good guy I'd sure be able to blackmail a few of these hifalutin' folks." Mike headed out with his armload. Our meeting was over.

"Well, thanks for the information Mike. I'm sure we'll be able to find out the names of Joan's partners."

"It shouldn't be hard. All you have to do is go to the tennis building and look them up. All the names are on the leaderboard. They've been having a summer tournament." He looked at Ginger. "I hope you pretty ladies find what you're looking for and don't get hurt in the process. It can be dangerous asking questions of a potential murderer." His unnerving grin sent chills up my spine.

He headed for the van while we went back across the field to the clubhouse. "What do ya' think, Gin?"

"I'm wondering how many of those tools are really his."

"Me too."

"He went between being helpful and creepy. Do you think he could have killed her?" I've found it hard to read people. I had leaned toward his innocence until he smiled that diabolical smile. I wasn't the only one who noticed.

"I really did think he was cute, but all that changed when he told us to be careful. That smile gave me the creeps." Ginger pulled her windblown hair from her face. "He did give us a good bit of information, though. Now all we have to do is get the names of the other girls on the team."

When we reached the clubhouse, I expected to see Honey and Miss Charlotte sitting on the patio where we'd left them. They were nowhere to be seen.

"Okay, where did they get off to?" I was concerned about Miss Charlotte's state of mind since finding her so forlorn this morning. I hoped she hadn't gone deeper into depression.

"Let's go inside and look," Ginger said.

I had no idea where to start. We looked in the dining room to find only a few lunch stragglers drinking coffee and eating dessert. The lobby was empty. On a whim I decided to check out the game room never expecting to find them there.

Honey and Miss Charlotte sat playing a game of cards. I hadn't seen Miss Charlotte laugh like that since – well I'm not sure I'd ever seen her laugh with such abandonment. A prick of jealousy stabbed my heart. Her doldrums had obviously disappeared while Ginger and I interviewed Mike.

I sat in one of the empty chairs and Ginger occupied the other. "What's so funny?"

"Oh, Skye. Honey is the cat's meow. I don't think I've ever laughed so hard. She's been telling me about her childhood in the Appalachian Mountains. She even told me some stories about Ginger."

Honey smiled at Ginger and started telling a long story about the two of them playing in the creek or some such place. I sat to listen, astonished at the chemistry developing between those three. If only I could be a part of that.

CHAPTER TWENTY-EIGHT

When Honey began a new story about a rabbit, Ginger tried to stop her. "Oh no, don't tell that one!"

Honey laughed so hard she gasped for breath. "I have to! It's the best. One time we were at the family pig roast and she came out of the house with nothing on but cotton balls stuck to her behind. She was jumping around saying, 'Look at me! I'm a bunny!'"

I couldn't help but join in the laughter when I pictured her hopping around the yard in her birthday suit. Even Miss Charlotte had tears rolling down her cheeks.

Ginger cracked a small smile. "Well, I hope y'all are having a good time. I was only three years old. I didn't know any better."

"Aw, come on Cuz'. You know I love you." Honey got up and gave Ginger a hug. "Of course you didn't know what you were doing. But you were the cutest thing hopping around with abandonment. Aunt Helen grabbed you up and rushed you back into the house. I do believe her face was a shade redder than a ripe tomato." This brought a smile to Ginger's face.

"Well, I don't remember much about it other than thinking I wanted to be like our pet rabbits."

I looked at my watch. It was already two o'clock. "If we're going to Candler this afternoon we'd better hit the road."

"How about the names we were going to look up?" Ginger reached over for Honey's tea.

Honey held it out of her reach. "Get your own tea. And what names, Skye? Did you find out anything from Mike?"

"Sure did. I'll tell you all about it on the way to Candler. I just have to make a stop by the tennis courts before we leave.

"I'm staying here, my feet are killing me and I want some sweet tea since Honey won't share." Ginger teased, but waved for a server to bring her a glass.

"I'll be back in a jiffy." I headed for the tennis courts alone.

It took me about ten minutes to find what I needed. The other three names on Joan's foursome: Penny Marshall, Tabitha Holbrook and Mindy Tolbert. I knew Penny and Tabitha, but wasn't familiar with Mindy. I could use the club directory to find their addresses and phone numbers.

The girls were ready to go when I returned to the patio. Honey attempted to help Miss Charlotte, but she pushed her hand away. She had a new spring in her step that wasn't there before. I believe Honey or maybe getting out and being included as one of the girls was just what the doctor ordered. I hoped this would be the beginning of bonding with Mitch's mother.

Traffic was heavier than usual for this time of day so the trip took longer than expected. I put the car in park and announced, "I need to go in and take some measurements. Ginger, would you grab that book of swatches in the back and bring it in?"

I started to suggest Miss Charlotte stay in the car, but thought she might like to be included. She might enjoy seeing the mansion. "Come on in, Miss Charlotte. I'd love for you to see the inside of this historic house. Maybe you could give us some pointers on keeping it authentic."

"Sure, come on, Lottie. Four heads are better than one." Honey chuckled as she helped Miss Charlotte out. She was always there to help Mitch's mother. I needed to be more attentive in the same way that came natural to Honey.

Honey grabbed one arm and I grabbed the other. She shook us off. "Oh, good grief, I'm not that feeble yet. Anyway, I brought my cane. I'll use it." She reached in the car and brought out a beautiful hand carved walking stick.

"That's some stick, Miss Charlotte," Ginger said.

Miss Charlotte smiled, "George had that made for me before he passed. It holds a special place in my heart." She straightened her back and walked as regally as she could. This was one proud lady.

Miss Charlotte surveyed the front room with interest. "This is very nice." She shook her head, "It's a shame the storm left so much damage. Why, look where the paper is coming right off the wall." She gave the wall a good poke with her walking stick.

The wall collapsed and an object rolled across the smooth hardwood floor from the shadows into the daylight. I shouldn't have been surprised when Miss Charlotte fainted, because I almost joined her when I saw it was a human skull!

CHAPTER TWENTY-NINE

"**O**h, my goodness! Would you look at that!" Ginger pointed to the hole. An arm devoid of flesh hung out of the wall and a headless skeleton was exposed to the waist. I assumed the rest was attached.

I knelt beside Miss Charlotte and took her pulse. *Lord, please don't let this be a heart attack. Think fast Skye.* "Ginger, could you wet some rags or paper towels in the kitchen and bring them to me?"

"Skye, I'm going to call Robert," Honey said. "He'll know what to do." She walked outside to make her call.

Ginger arrived with a handful of wet paper towels. I dabbed the cooling liquid across her forehead. Ginger fanned her hand back and forth over Miss Charlotte's face. I was dialing 911 when she slowly opened her eyes. "Who? What?" She struggled to sit up.

"I don't know Miss Charlotte. It seems there was a skeleton in the wall. When you poked it with your walking stick it opened up a hole and the skeleton's head rolled across the floor. I'm so sorry you had to see that." Actually, I was sorry any of us had to be witness to such a sight.

"I swanny, Skye, do you always attract trouble everywhere you go?" Well, she obviously felt better. Back to throwing daggers at me.

I examined the rooms furnishings, "Miss Charlotte, I surely didn't expect this to happen. How about we get you up and into one of these chairs." With Ginger's help we stood her and Gin quickly shoved a chair beneath her.

The door opened, grabbing everyone's attention. "Robert said he was in the middle of a crime scene and couldn't get away. He's going to call Detective Haynes." Honey plopped in one of the abandoned chairs, crossed her arms and huffed. "I'd rather have Robert come."

I would, too, because I knew Detective Haynes wouldn't be happy we'd unearthed a body. The chances were high it was a murder victim because who'd bury a body in the wall if it wasn't?

Soon, we heard the detective's car roll into the driveway. He unfolded his lanky body as he disembarked from the driver's side. I opened the door for him. He came inside, followed by two uniformed officers.

He tipped his hat, "Is everyone all right? Do we need a paramedic unit?"

"I think we're fine except for the shock," I told him.

"I received a strange call from Detective Montaine. Something about a runaway skeleton head."

I pointed to the corner where it rested, and showed him the remainder of the exposed body in the wall. He removed his hat and swiped at his forehead with a white handkerchief. He replaced his fedora, similar to ones I'd seen them wear on the news. I wondered if it was a tradition among Atlanta detectives.

He rubbed his chin. "Interesting to say the least. Seems like y'all attract trouble." He gave the officers some orders and began writing in a small notebook.

Miss Charlotte couldn't agree fast enough. "That's exactly what I told Skye."

I resisted the temptation to roll my eyes. "Well, I certainly didn't plan this. Remember, I came here with the intention of working." I turned to the detective. "Don't you think it's connected to an old murder? Why conceal the body in a wall unless you had something to hide?"

"You're probably right. And this is now considered a crime scene until we process everything. I'll have to ask y'all to vacate the premises until further notice."

I thought of the work needed to be done to stay on schedule. "What about my work?"

"I'll call and let you know when we've finished. It could be as early as tomorrow."

I was anxious to start working on the house, but the discovery of the skeleton piqued my interest. Who were the previous owners?

We gathered our supplies and helped Miss Charlotte back to the car. She didn't resist this time. "Oh, my! I will have to tell Mitch about this. He won't believe it," she said. Then she looked at me. "Or maybe he will." I ignored the stab and helped her into the front seat.

"I need to get back and get ready for my date with Robert," Honey said.

I was happy Honey had found a beau to fill the void of her late husband. It dawned on me Miss Charlotte must be lonely as well. I should learn to cut her some slack and surround her with friends. I looked in the rearview at Ginger. "Gin, would you like to have supper with us? Mitch or I could run you home after we eat."

"No thanks. I think I'll go home and relax. After today I could use a little quiet time. I'll take a rain check though." I thought I heard Miss Charlotte breathe a sigh of relief.

"Okay, I'll hold you to it. In the meantime, I've got this great idea. Since we can't work on the house tomorrow how about we track down the previous owners. Maybe we can help solve the mystery of the skeleton?"

Honey said yes while Ginger and Miss Charlotte chimed in with no at the same time. At least they'd finally agreed on something.

"You don't need to get mixed up in this, Skye. As Mitch's mother, I'm telling you he will not like it one bit!"

"I have to agree with Miss Charlotte. Don't we have enough on our plates trying to solve Joan's murder?" *Now* Ginger agrees with Miss Charlotte.

"I'm dying to know as well. It'll be a piece of cake to figure out who owned the house, it won't take long," Honey said.

I perked up with Honey on my side. "I agree. I thought we could start tomorrow at the tax assessor's office on Commerce looking at past deeds. I think we can track all the way back to the original owners. Honey, you and I've done some work there before."

"I'd love it. We can get an early start if I don't stay out too late with Magnum, oops, I mean Robert." Honey's laughter filled the car. It was nice to have a little comic relief.

Honey, in a hurry to get beautiful for her date, took off as soon as we arrived back at the condo. I noticed Mitch's car in the garage. Why was he home so early?

CHAPTER THIRTY

"I see Mitchell is home. What an adventure I have to tell him."

What a great way to look at it. "You're right Miss Charlotte, it was quite an adventure. One I don't want to experience any time soon. I have to admit, getting mixed up in these murder cases makes me feel like I'm in a Hallmark Mystery Movie Series. It's kind of exciting."

"Maybe it's not your fault you attract dead people."

I gave Miss Charlotte a smile. I think she was teasing, but I chose to take it as a compliment that she was finally more comfortable around me. Maybe my patience plus persistence would pay off in the long run. Mitch and Buddy met us at the door. I scooped up Buddy so he wouldn't trip Miss Charlotte again. I didn't want a repeat of last night. Had it only been last night when she fell?

Buddy rewarded me with a lick on the face and Mitch planted a kiss on my lips.

"What are you doing home?"

"Well, hello to you, too," Mitch said. "Can't a guy surprise his two best girls with dinner out?" Mitch rescued Buddy from my arms while I helped Miss Charlotte to the recliner.

"Oh, Mitch, darling. I appreciate your gesture, but I don't think I feel up to going out tonight. I'm sure Skye won't mind cooking." Actually, I didn't feel like going out either.

"Sure. I don't mind. Why don't we eat in tonight, honey, and I'll whip up a good ole' southern meal? How about chicken fried steak and mashed potatoes?"

"Yum, sounds good!"

He reached over and whispered, "thank you," in my ear as he gave me a big hug.

I had supper ready and on the table in forty-five minutes. After we sat down to eat, Miss Charlotte didn't waste time telling Mitch about the run-away skeleton head.

"Well, at least this is one they can't pin on you or the girls. I'm just glad it isn't something you'll get mixed up in."

I was surprised when Miss Charlotte didn't spill the beans about Honey and I looking for the past owners of the house. I didn't agree or disagree with Mitch – I just kept silent and nodded. No need to worry him unnecessarily.

The evening passed quickly. Miss Charlotte went to bed early. Mitch and I spent some quality time together and I even wore my pink teddy.

I welcomed morning after a night filled with dreams of a headless skeleton chasing me around the old house on Candler.

I opened the door and Buddy shot out like a bullet. To my surprise the sun shone bright as a copper penny, after a night of steady rain. The azaleas blazed red and pink in the sunlight. The bushes popped with shades of green. God's handiwork shone everywhere.

Mitch had left early so it was just me and Miss Charlotte for breakfast. We had just finished when the doorbell rang. The giant smile on Honey's face was a dead give-away she'd had a great night with Detective Hunky.

"Well, somebody looks happy this morning," I said.

"Sugar, I'm as happy as a frog on a lily pad. We had a wonderful time last night. I think he might be number three, Skye."

I wouldn't be surprised if he was. Honey's outfit reflected her mood. She wore bright orange Capris paired with a white tee and a yellow vest, with fringe decorating the front, reminding me of a cowgirl.

Ginger wore denim Capris matched with a modest pullover. Maybe Honey had finally influenced Ginger's style of dressing. This would be another big step in her rehabilitation. I wore my usual Khaki pants and white tee, but I'd spruced it up with a bright teal necklace.

Miss Charlotte had dressed in her familiar uniform. A dark dress with stockings and pearls. "Lottie, why don't you put on a pair of pants? You'll be a lot more comfortable. You don't know what we might get ourselves into today," Honey said.

I expected her to balk at Honey's suggestion.

"I did bring a pair of dress slacks, but I've only worn them once. Just didn't feel right."

Honey grabbed her by the arm and guided her toward her room. "We'll wait right here for you."

While she changed, we discussed the agenda for the day. Since I hadn't heard anything from Detective Haynes I assumed we wouldn't be allowed in the house to work. I suggested we do something fun after we'd talked to one of Joan's tennis partners.

"Don't forget we wanted to research the deeds on the house, too."

I couldn't remember seeing Miss Charlotte wearing pants. Yes, they were black dress pants paired with a lacy white blouse and her signature pearl necklace, but it was a great start to getting her to loosen up a little.

"Don't you look nice?" The compliment sprang from my heart. Could I grow to love this lady? I determined right then and there to give it my best.

She smiled. "Thank you."

I gave Buddy a dog bone and scratch behind the ears. He headed for what was becoming his favorite spot under the window where the sun warmed the floor.

"Come on girls! We have a full day ahead of us and we don't want to miss a minute of daylight," Honey said. She led the way and I followed after locking the door behind us.

I suggested we call Penny first, since we'd been on several committees together. "She's giving tennis lessons and won't be through until eleven. She wants to meet us at the club for lunch. I guess it won't hurt to eat there two days in a row."

"Oh, my! And I'm wearing pants," Miss Charlotte said.

"Don't you worry about a thing, Miss Charlotte, you're wearing dress pants. You'll still be dressed up." Honey reached up and patted her shoulder. "And don't forget your pearls."

"I've got an idea. Let's head over to the tax assessor's office while we're waiting on Penny to finish up."

"I don't think it's such a good idea," Ginger said. "I have enough to worry about without worrying about some ole' skeleton."

"Me neither," concurred Miss Charlotte.

You're in hot water now, Skye. You'd better think of something quick.

CHAPTER THIRTY-ONE

"We don't all have to go. Why don't I drop y'all off at the Java Monkey while we conduct our research?" Maybe this would be a good time for Gin and Miss Charlotte to bond, if they didn't kill each other first.

"What's this *Java Monkey?* Sounds like where monkeys go to drink coffee," Miss Charlotte announced.

Laughter filled the car. Miss Charlotte sat up a little straighter. "What's so funny about that?"

"It's a coffee shop located close to Decatur Square. It's where all the *in* crowd goes. You'll love it Lottie."

"Well, if you say so, Honey." Of course, it was all right if Honey approved.

I let them off, hoping they'd be in one piece when we returned.

"Honey, I appreciate you and Gin helping with Mitch's mother. I don't think I could handle her alone. She's experienced depression since George died, and I've seen it first-hand since she's stayed with us. I don't know what to do except try and keep her busy. Maybe take her mind off it." I glanced at Honey, "That's why I told Mitch I'd take her with us."

"I think it's a good idea. I like Lottie, she's just stuck in a different time."

"You can say that again!" I looked at Honey, "but don't."

"There!" Honey shouted.

I slammed on the brakes. "There what?" Honey nearly burst my eardrum not to mention scaring the bejeebers out of me.

"A parking place." She pointed to a spot along the street.

Wasn't I lucky?

She shot me a smile. "I know it's parallel, but I have confidence you can do it." I parked like a pro after only two tries.

We entered the tax office and were greeted by a gray-haired lady who'd probably worked there for years. "Hello, ladies, I'm Doris. What can I do for you?" A smile spread across her face, and her wrinkles rearranged themselves.

Honey and I spoke at the same time.

She held up a hand. "Whoa there. One at a time please."

"We'd like to look up the owners of an old house please."

She showed us a cubby available for research. An hour later we'd discovered the house had been built in 1895 by Frederick McGuire. Honey and I slapped our palms together in a high-five.

Doris witnessed our display of excitement. "Did you find what you're looking for?"

"We sure did. Do you know if Frederick McGuire was related to the family who owned McGuire's Emporium during the early 1900's?"

"Honey, do I look that old?" Doris' witty comeback sparked laughter from us.

I sputtered, trying to cover my faux pa. "Of course not! I thought you might have information on some of the local historic landmarks."

"I don't, but try the Special Collections at the DeKalb County Library. There might be some newspaper articles or other information available. Janice can help you."

I looked at my watch. "Oh my goodness, look at the time. We'd better hurry, Honey."

"And don't forget we're supposed to meet Penny for lunch," Honey said.

I turned to Doris. "Thank you so much for your help. We'll check out the library." We hurried to the car where I made a quick getaway. I wove in and out of traffic reaching the Java Monkey with time to spare. I whipped in the only place left on the square. When I entered the coffee shop, I didn't expect to see Ginger and Miss Charlotte, heads close together, engaged in animated conversation.

Ginger spotted us and waved. "Glad to see y'all made it back. We'd begun to think you'd gone to lunch without us." Ginger raised her coffee cup draining the last few drops. "That was good!" She wiped her mouth with the back of her hand.

"Yes, it was," Miss Charlotte concurred. "I'm glad you suggested this place, Skye. Ginger and I had an enlightening conversation. She told me all about the life of an exotic dancer."

Heat warmed my face, as I struggled to slow my breathing. I'm sure Miss Charlotte couldn't wait to relay this to Mitch.

"And I heard all about Lottie's life." Ginger pointed to two empty chairs at the next table. "Sit." We dragged them over. "I explained how Honey took me into her home and you'd given me a job so I'd have an opportunity to turn my life around." She reached over and patted her cousin's hand. "I'm so grateful for both of you believing in me and giving me a chance for a better life. I told Miss Charlotte I know I have a lot to learn, but I'm not the same girl I was a year ago." She grabbed both our hands, "And I have y'all to thank for that."

I remembered when Ginger came to stay with Honey and how skeptical I'd been. Not only had Ginger grown, but so had I. I'd learned you can't judge a book by its cover. Ginger had given it one hundred percent and I'd witnessed a beautiful transformation.

I squeezed her hand. "I'm so glad you came to stay with Honey."

"This mushy stuff is all good, but if we're going to make it to our date with Penny we need to be on the way," Honey said.

"I'll run and get the car and pick y'all up," I grabbed my keys from my purse.

"No! I want to walk, Skye." Miss Charlotte stood and grasped her walking stick. "I need the exercise."

I hesitated, but decided the fresh air might do her good. I hoped it didn't flare up her pain. We made good time and pulled into the club ten minutes before our meeting. Penny had changed out of her tennis outfit into shorts and a sleeveless tee. She sat at one of the tables drinking tea. She spotted our troop and waved us over.

CHAPTER THIRTY-TWO

"Hello, ladies." Penny turned to me, "Skye, what's this all about?"

My heart sped up and my palms moistened with sweat when the inevitable approached. "Penny." All eyes focused on me. "We're here to ask you some questions about Joan Smith."

Her smile faded. "Yes?"

"I don't know if you've heard, but the police took Ginger in for questioning and we're trying to help her out of this mess." I silently prayed Penny would cooperate – obviously not in time.

Penny placed her tea glass on the table, leaned in and stared me down. "The way I heard it, Daniel was arrested for her murder. Serves him right the way he treated her." She eyed Ginger with disdain. Evidently, Joan wasn't the only one who didn't want her as a club member.

A stab of guilt pricked my heart. Less than a year ago, I probably would've assumed the same. Ginger possessed more brass than class, but that didn't make her less of a person. I was so thankful God had opened my eyes and allowed me to see how much I needed to grow.

Honey cleared her throat. "Where'd you go, Skye? Penny asked you a question."

"I'm sorry. I drifted a minute." Penny's fingertips tap danced on the table. "Now what were you saying?"

"I said." She looked at Ginger, "I don't really know her and who's to say she didn't kill Joan. I was in the dining room when she threatened her. The whole team heard. Anyway, I've already told that detective about it." She sat back, crossed her arms and smiled smugly.

"Ginger didn't *threaten*, Joan. I was there, too, you know." Chalk one up for the Gipper. "By the way, aren't you president of the Decatur Garden Club?"

"Yes I am. What's that got to do with Joan's death?" Penny broke off a piece of bread and popped it into her mouth.

"Joan was poisoned with a pesticide." Penny dropped her remaining bread. "I'm sure you have ready availability to all kinds of weed killer." Her eyes grew wide and drops of sweat beaded on her upper lip. "A little birdy told me there wasn't any love lost between you and Joan," I said.

"Who told you such a thing?" Her face shone tomato red.

"It doesn't matter," I said. "The important thing is you disliked, Joan. Am I right?"

"So – just about everybody at the club has been subjected to her sharp tongue at one time or another. She had more enemies than friends," Penny said. "I'd be bitter, too, if my husband was a philanderer and didn't care who knew it. I never did understand why she stayed with him. Sometimes there's no rhyme or reason to a relationship." She dabbed at her forehead with the cloth napkin. "I felt sorry for her more than anything."

Honey jumped in. "Speaking of relationships, is it true Mindy Tolbert was having an affair with Daniel?"

Miss Charlotte gasped and looked at Honey like she'd lost her ever-loving mind. She turned a nice shade of pink, grabbed a paper menu and started fanning. I'd say it was safe to wager this was her first murder investigation.

"Humph! You'll have to ask her that yourself." Penny got up. "Well, I've got to be somewhere in a few minutes so this conversation is over. If I'd known you were going to imply I had something to do with Joan's death I surely wouldn't have invited you for lunch. She stood and reached for her purse; holding it in plain sight she thrust it toward us. You need to be careful asking these kind of questions.

She left in a huff.

This was the second time we'd been warned to be careful. My gut told me we were on to something like a hound dog on a coon's trail.

"My word girls, do you have to ask such personal questions?" Miss Charlotte fanned as fast as a hummingbird's wings. She downed the rest of her tea and continued fanning.

Honey chuckled. "Lottie, we have to be thorough. Remember, we're trying to help Ginger and if we want to get to the truth we have to be blunt."

"Did you see her wield her purse like she had a gun in it or something? It felt a lot like a threat to me," Ginger declared.

Thanks, Gin. Give Miss Charlotte more reasons to complain to Mitch about me. I steered the conversation in another direction. "Look, we've been stretched to our limit, like a twisted rubber band, for the past several days. Let's do something fun!"

"That's a great idea!" Honey agreed. "Fernbank is having a special exhibit on creatures of light. You know, things like lightening bugs and such. It's been years since I've been there. I'd love to see the exhibits again.

"I'm in." I addressed Miss Charlotte and Ginger. "How about y'all?"

Ginger danced in place. "I'd love to go. One day I'm going to be cultured like you and Honey."

And I believed her. "Since we're all in agreement let's ditch this joint and head over to Fernbank."

Honey helped Miss Charlotte up. "Come on Lottie. We have places to go and things to do."

CHAPTER THIRTY-THREE

ernbank Museum of Natural History is located on Clifton Road, east of Midtown. I dropped the girls off at the front door and drove to the parking deck. I hoped Miss Charlotte felt like walking. If getting a little exercise diminished her doldrums even a little, it would be worth the extra effort.

Honey had already bought tickets and they were waiting for me in the lobby. "Come on, Skye. We don't have all day. The museum closes at five."

"All right." We went into a large open area occupied by two giant brass dinosaur replicas.

"Wow, look at that!" Ginger craned her neck upward to view the head of an *Argentinosaurus*. Named so because it was discovered in Argentina. According to the museum brochure it weighed over a hundred tons and was the length of four school buses.

The museum offered more displays than we'd be able to finish in one day. We especially enjoyed the exhibit on the creatures of light. After viewing the Dinosaur Gallery, we decided we had time to tour one more exhibit. Miss Charlotte insisted on the Okefenokee Swamp. A disaster I didn't see coming. Miss Charlotte slowed to a stop halfway through the exhibit.

"Getting tired? Want us to wait while you rest a minute?" Maybe we'd pushed her too hard.

"No. No. I'm fine. I just need to catch my breath," Miss Charlotte said. "You girls go ahead and I'll catch up."

We walked a little ways and stopped, giving her time to recover. It couldn't have been more than five minutes when I heard Miss Charlotte screaming, "I broke it! I broke it!"

Rushing back to the display where we'd left her I found her sitting on the other side of the wooden railing cradling her hand. I thanked God she was still alive, but it didn't keep me from wanting to strangle her with my bare hands.

I climbed over the fence as fast as a fifty-something woman could. "Gin, go get an employee."

"I'll call 911," Honey said as she rummaged for her cell.

My attention returned to Miss Charlotte. "What in the world are you doing on this side of the rail?" Tears pooled in her eyes, but I was too mad to feel empathetic. Why would she do such a foolish thing?

She sniffed. "I was standing there looking at the display when I noticed one of the ducks turned over. I figured since I had on pants I could climb over and fix it. I lost my balance and fell on my hand. I think it's broke." Supporting her hand, she thrust it toward me. A big blue bruise had already formed on her wrist.

Ginger returned with a female guard in tow. She waited with us until the EMT's wrapped Miss Charlotte's hand and transferred her to the ambulance. They told us they would transport her to Emory, the closest hospital. We assured a distraught Miss Charlotte we'd follow in the car.

Before leaving, the guard escorted me to the office where I filled out a plethora of paperwork. It was obvious they were concerned about liability, but I didn't see any on their part since Miss Charlotte willingly climbed over the fence erected to keep tourists out of the displays.

The girls and I left before the ink dried. What would Mitch say when he found out his mother broke her wrist? *Dear Lord please let it be sprained and not broken.* Distracted, speeding to the hospital, I turned left in front of a semi-truck. Thankfully we weren't pulled over by the police or worse – killed.

I pulled in a space, slammed the gear in park and hopped out the door yelling, "Every man for himself." James A. Andrews, notorious train robber delivered the famous quote while his gang was being pursued. Unfortunately, he was captured and hung.

The young woman behind the desk looked up when she saw me running toward her. "Is there an emergency?" And yes, she was blonde even if it was a dye job. And not a very good one at that.

My nerves got the better of me, "This is the emergency room isn't it?" She returned my sarcastic remark with a dazed look. "We're here for Miss Charlotte. She came in by ambulance."

"And what would Miss Charlotte's last name be?" A pink bubble emerged from the receptionist's mouth. She sucked it back in and continued smacking. I wanted to reach across the desk and pull that gum right out of her mouth.

Honey read my mind. She laid a comforting hand on my shoulder. "No need to cause a scene, Skye." She addressed Blondie, "Her last name is Southerland – Charlotte Southerland."

Thank you God for friends like Honey. I could be sitting in a jail cell right now over a piece of bubble gum.

She punched some keys on the computer, blew a few more bubbles, and wrote a number on a sticky pad. She handed me the piece of paper. "Here ya' go. *Miss Charlotte* is in examining room six. I'll buzz you in."

In all the commotion I'd forgotten to call Mitch. I decided to check on her status first. Miss Charlotte lay stiff as a board, covered to her chin with her eyes closed. *She's dead!*

CHAPTER THIRTY-FOUR

"Miss Charlotte?"

"Lottie?"

Ginger leaned next to Miss Charlotte's ear and used her outside voice, "Ms. Southerland!"

Big brown eyes popped open. "Goodness. What is it?" She looked at Ginger, "I'm quite sure you woke the dead."

Little did she know we'd thought she was one of them. "We just wanted to make sure you were all right. What did the doctor say?"

"Is it broken?" Ginger raised the sheet to take a peek at the injured limb.

Miss Charlotte grabbed at the sheet with her other hand. "I'm waiting on the doctor to read the x-rays. They said it could take up to an hour – or more."

There was nothing else to do but hurry up and wait. I took the opportunity to call Mitch. He reached the hospital in twenty minutes.

Mitch walked over to his mother's side. With a shaky voice he asked, "What happened?"

"Well, dear, after Skye interviewed a murder suspect, she suggested we go to Fernbank Museum." Mitch nodded, but cut a glance over at me. "We were in the Okefenokee exhibit and next thing I knew I'd fallen and hurt my wrist." Tears slid down her cheeks. "I think it's broken." I didn't have the heart to tell Mitch how she'd climbed over the fence. I'd tell him later.

The doctor walked in, followed by a nurse, saving me from Mitch's scrutiny. I was sure I'd be interrogated later. "Hi, I'm Doctor Williams."

The nurse surveyed our crew and declared only two visitors to a room, so Honey and Ginger retreated to the waiting room. "Ms. Southerland, I have good news and bad news." The doctor cleared his throat. "The bad news is your wrist is broken. The good news is; you won't require surgery. We can cast it and you'll be good as new in about four weeks. You can even pick out your favorite color."

Broken? Mitch and I groaned at the same time. What else could go wrong during Miss Charlotte's visit? I plopped into a visitor's chair as exhaustion overwhelmed me.

"My PA will be in to cast your wrist. You're already in the casting room so you won't have to move." He gingerly patted her shoulder. "I'll write you a prescription for pain meds and when she's done you can go home. Be sure and elevate your arm to keep the swelling down."

Miss Charlotte decided on a white cast declaring it would match whatever she wore. I wasn't surprised – I couldn't picture her wearing a hot pink or purple cast.

The girls jumped up when we entered the waiting room. "Oh, Miss Charlotte, look at your arm. You were right – you did break your wrist. Wow, it's almost to your elbow," Ginger said.

I wanted to get Miss Charlotte home so she could rest. "Come on girls, I'll take you back to the house to get your car. I think we're ready to call it a night." The ride home was unusually quiet. It had been a long day.

Honey and Ginger said good-night and headed to their house. By the time I settled Miss Charlotte in the recliner it was going on eight, way past suppertime. I cooked a quick cheese omelet for each of us. Miss Charlotte picked at hers. I gobbled mine down faster than a Gecko hunting shade on a summer day.

I helped Mitch's mother get dressed for bed. Bless her heart, she was having a little trouble maneuvering her arm. I had confidence it would get better as the pain subsided. By the time I'd hung up her clothes and straightened the room she was softly snoring.

Mitch sat in his recliner, hidden behind the paper. I could see his eyes as it slowly descended. "Honey, I'm not mad, I just need to know what happened."

I swallowed the lump stuck in my throat. "We decided to have some fun so we drove to Fernbank to see the new exhibit." Mitch turned down the TV.

"Her fall didn't happen exactly the way she led you to believe," I said.

"How did it happen?" Mitch laid the paper in his lap and gave me his full attention.

"She stopped to rest and told us to walk ahead and she'd catch up. We'd only walked a short way, when I heard her screaming. I ran back and found her on the other side of the safety fence. She fell while climbing over it to fix a display." Tears filled my eyes.

Mitch patted his leg, "Aww, come here honey." I sat on his lap and he wrapped his arms around me. His loving embrace was all it took to open the floodgates. A good cry is what I needed. The pressure valve released some of the stress from the past few weeks.

"Is that all?"

I confessed to digging in the murder case some more.

Mitch rubbed my back in a circular motion, "After today I think it'd be better if she stayed here. Especially if you insist on poking your nose in murder cases. It could get dangerous, you know. I'd tell you not to, but it would be like talking to a fencepost."

"You're right. I'll make sure she's comfortable."

Mitch kissed my cheek, "I'm glad you see it my way. You have plenty to keep busy with at work and as a new dog owner."

Buddy thumped his tail on the floor and laid his chin on my lap. His big brown eyes comforted me. I was one lucky girl.

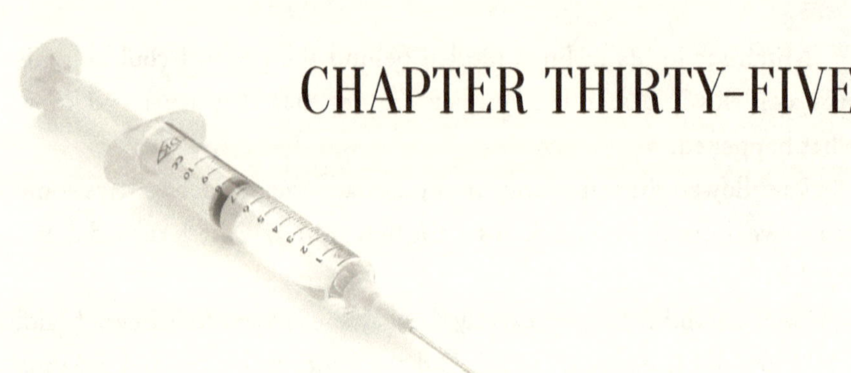

CHAPTER THIRTY-FIVE

ednesday brought rain and gray skies. I wanted to curl up, pull the covers over my head and go back to sleep. But I remembered Miss Charlotte now sported a cast and needed tending. I heard Buddy whimpering outside my bedroom door and knew he needed attention as well.

I said a prayer and asked for strength to face today's challenges. The thought entered my mind, I so often asked for this and for that and forgot to be thankful for all my blessings. I said a second prayer of thanksgiving.

Miss Charlotte was sound asleep when I checked in on her. The pain medicine must be working. I decided to wait and wake her for breakfast. I cooked a stack of pancakes. I figured Miss Charlotte and I could use some comfort food – piping hot pancakes drenched in melted butter covered with Alaga, sugar cane, syrup.

The girls showed up before I had breakfast on the table. I still wore my robe and hadn't even touched my hair. I finger-combed my short mane knowing it probably wouldn't help.

Rain blew in when I opened the door. "Good morning, Skye. You look like something Buddy dragged in last night." Honey laughed and Ginger followed her lead. I didn't laugh, but I moved aside so they could come in out of the rain.

"I was awake off and on all night with Miss Charlotte. I'm fixing to wake her for breakfast. Want some pancakes?"

"Got any Alaga?" Honey smacked her lips.

"Sure do," I said.

"I'd love some, too." Ginger called over her shoulder as she took their dripping raincoats to hang up in the bathroom.

"Look, I need to talk with y'all before Miss Charlotte gets up. You know she'll need to stay home because of her arm. Anyway, Mitch didn't want her getting mixed up in the investigation into Joan's murder. I'm not sure I'll be able to go with y'all unless I hire someone to sit with her."

Ginger grabbed the plates and took them to the table. "Why don't I stay with Miss Charlotte while you and Honey do your sleuthing? She's not so bad, you just have to get to know her."

"You sure, Gin? That would be a big help."

"Sure, I'm sure. I'm getting to really like hearing about her younger days, and Mitch's childhood."

That stung a little, and I vowed to make more of an effort. After all, she'd raised my awesome husband, so she had to have something going for her.

I woke Miss Charlotte for breakfast and we stuffed ourselves with pancakes and bacon. Ginger stacked the dishes while Honey helped Miss Charlotte get dressed, and I went upstairs to clean up. Thirty minutes later we were ready to walk out the door.

"Ginger, you've got my cell number and she won't need another pain pill until noon. Buddy will let you know if he has to go outside. Call me if you need anything."

"Will do. Don't you worry about us none. We'll be fine." She offered me a reassuring grin.

The rain had stopped, but clouds dotted the sky. I hoped it'd clear up soon. Gray days often left me in a funk.

"Hey, Skye, want to ride in the Crossfire today?"

I hesitated.

"With cold weather coming, it might be a while before you get another chance," Honey said.

I surely didn't want to miss out on a chance to zip in and out of speeding traffic. "Okay, let's live dangerously."

"Very funny, Skye. Come on, it'll be fun."

We discussed which mystery to work on first, Joan's murder or the one of the headless skeleton. Honey suggested we visit Mindy Tolbert, the girl Mike said was having an affair with Daniel.

"You're not going to believe where she works." I didn't give Honey a chance to answer. "The Botanical Gardens."

"You're kidding," Honey said.

I shook my head. "I don't kid about people who work with pesticides."

"Then she has access to the same kind of poison that killed Joan. It's bizarre all these people happen to have pesticides available to them."

"Like Daniel said, almost everybody has access. All they'd have to do is to go the garden store and purchase it. We have to find a strong enough motive for somebody to kill her," I said.

"We'll just have to flush them out," Honey said.

Fortunately, we didn't have to get on the freeway to reach the Gardens. I made it with my nerves still intact. Visiting the gardens flooded my mind with unwanted memories. At the beginning of summer, Honey, Ginger and I had decided to check out the Niki de Saint Phalle mosaic exhibit. While standing on the edge of the water fountain waiting for Honey to take my picture, I slipped and fell in. Not only was it embarrassing, but I had to ride home soaked. To top it off, we missed the rest of the exhibit.

It was gone now, replaced with Chihuly in the Gardens exhibit. "Look Honey, there's a staff member. Let's ask her where Mindy works."

"I sure do know Mindy Tolbert. She's head of our vegetable gardening program. You'll find her either in the garden working or in her office located in the garden shop." He gestured toward a quaint cottage. "Over there."

A kaleidoscope of colors burst along the pathway: yellow, red, pink, and even salmon color roses emitted a heavenly scent. Another blessing to be thankful for.

By the time we reached the vegetable garden the sun had decided to favor us with golden rays. A gift shop designed to look like a cute little house sat to the side of the garden. Several people were shopping for gardening materials or gifts.

A cute redhead waltzed over to where Honey and I looked at tools. "May I help you?" She nodded toward a trowel I held. "Those are on sale today."

"Actually, we're looking for Mindy Tolbert," I said.

"I'm Mindy. What can I do for you?"

Honey didn't pull any punches. "We'd like to ask you some questions about Joan Smith's murder."

She grabbed the trowel from my hand and shoved it back on the shelf.

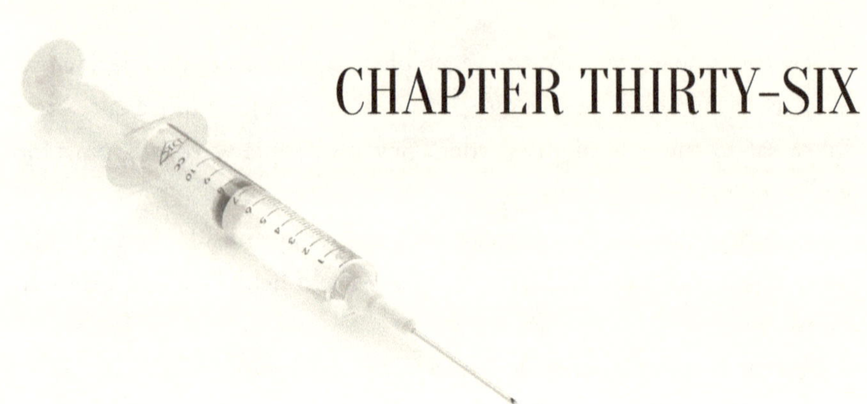

CHAPTER THIRTY-SIX

Mindy quickly looked around and whispered, "Come in my office. I'm not going to talk out here." She led us into a nice sized room with a wall of windows welcoming the sun.

She planted herself in a plush office chair behind an elegant Cherrywood desk. It was evident she had surrounded herself with nice things. She pulled the over-sized chair up to the desk and leaned her elbows on it, reminding me of a kid wanting to play grown-up.

I shut the door behind us and Honey and I sat on a pair of folding chairs. The elegance obviously didn't extend to visitors.

"What do you think I could tell you that I didn't tell the police?" Mindy eyed me then Honey.

I jumped right in. "Did you have an affair with Daniel Smith?"

"Of course not." She bound her long red hair into a ponytail. "Sure, we flirted with each other and went out for dinner and drinks a couple of times, but that's as far as it went. He said he was trying to decide whether he wanted to stay with his wife. Likely story. I think I intimidated him."

Honey sat up straighter. "You knew he was married?"

"Didn't seem to bother your cousin." She looked at Honey, "Yeah, I know all about her little tryst with Daniel. I was in the dining room the day she argued with Joan. Seems to me the police are on the right trail going after her."

"Humph," Honey snorted. "Everybody has something to hide, dear. And as for Ginger, she didn't know Daniel was married."

Mindy stood, "I have work to do." She hurried around the desk and jerked open the door. We didn't need to be rocket scientists to know she wasn't giving up any more information. As we hurried out, she hissed, "And don't come back to my work place."

"She sure has a chip on her shoulder," Honey said as we scooted away toward the parking lot.

"Yeah, what did you think about her story? Was she telling the truth about not having an affair with Daniel?" I inhaled heavens' sweet scent as we passed through the rose garden.

"She's hiding something. It was written all over her face." Honey stopped and fingered the velvety rose pedals. "What if Daniel really was trying to be faithful and she was in love with him. She could have killed Joan to get her out of the way."

"It would seem extreme just to get a man, but I've learned people will kill for crazier reasons. So, if you ask me, I'd have to say it's possible and definitely keeps her on the list."

I gave the fountain a cursory look as we exited the gardens. Nothing but bad memories there.

"Hey, Skye, want to drive topless? Now the sun's out it should be warm enough. With cold weather around the corner, we need to enjoy it while we can." She started the process before I answered.

I didn't worry so much about my hair blowing ever since I'd gotten it cut short, and it was a beautiful day.

She got behind the wheel and pulled the rearview mirror towards her. She whipped out her lipstick, colored her lips and smacked, "Lookin' good girl!"

I had to admit she did.

Honey noticed me watching, "Come on, Skye, try some. I promise you'll love it."

I'd never had the nerve to wear red lipstick, but the Merle Norman shade did look great on Honey. "Since I'm living dangerously today, let's go for it."

"Yippee!" She handed me the stick and turned the rearview towards me.

I adjusted it where I could see my lips. I bit the bullet and swiped the creamy lipstick on. I smacked my lips and turned to show her. "Not bad. Do you think Mitch will like it?" I took another look and noticed how the color brightened my face.

"Wow! He'll love it." She winked. "I know Robert does."

"I guess I'll have to get some then. Maybe we can swing by the Merle Norman shop and I can buy my own. I could use a little pick-me-up."

Honey laughed and started the car. "Where shall we eat lunch?"

"Tabitha Holbrook lives in Avondale. Why don't we stop at Avondale Pizza? My treat."

"Sounds good to me." She revved the engine, backed out, and gunned it.

I've always loved this part of Atlanta. A little country in the big city. The terrain flew by as Honey scooted down the road. We hit the lunch crowd, but luckily found an open table. The atmosphere at the café rivaled the food.

The tables were covered with red and white checked tablecloths. A small lantern provided a majestic glow to the table. The red brick walls added ambiance to the café. It was our lucky day, the waiter sat us in front of the open brick oven. Premier seating.

"Let's get a Hawaiian pizza," Honey said.

"Sounds good to me. What's not to like about ham and pineapple?" After the waitress brought out drinks and took our order, we sat back to wait. I picked up a brochure on the local area.

CHAPTER THIRTY-SEVEN

I took a sip of tea and skimmed the first paragraphs. "This tells the history of Avondale. Listen: '*The City of Avondale Estates was founded by George Francis Willis in 1924. Willis' plans for the City were inspired by the trip he and his wife, Lottie, had taken to Stratford-upon-Avon, England. He aspired to recreate the majestic Tudor-Revival style architecture found at the birthplace of William Shakespeare.*'"

"So that's where Avondale got its name?" Honey grabbed a brochure. "I'd like to read this later."

"It's interesting." I pointed to the brochure. "The first Waffle House was opened in 1955 in Avondale. It's a museum now located on East College Avenue. Maybe we can visit it when we have more time." I folded the pamphlet.

After the waitress left our pizza and we'd grabbed our first piece, Honey continued our conversation. "Does Tabitha know we're coming?"

"I called her last night and she said she'd be home all afternoon."

"What reason did you give her for coming?" Honey blew her pizza trying to cool it.

"I told her we wanted to talk to her about working on a committee at the club." Honey shook her head. "Well, I know I fudged a little, but I am the Chair for the Fall Festival Committee. I'm going to ask her to help."

"You stretched that one a little. Hopefully, she won't clam up after we veer off the trail and bring up Daniel and Joan." Honey took a big bite. "Yum!"

I followed her lead. "Or maybe we can tell something about her involvement if we play it really cool." I wiped pizza sauce off my chin.

We left nothing but crumbs on the pizza tin. We got a take-out pizza for Ginger and headed over to Ohm Street where Tabitha lived. Her house, a little white cottage, was surrounded with summer flowers. Azaleas filled the yard while colorful flower beds surrounded the trees and decorated the front of the house.

"Somebody's put a lot of work into the landscaping. I wonder who their gardener is." Honey no sooner asked the question when Tabitha rounded the corner. Wearing gardening gloves, she held a flat of pansies.

"Hi, Skye. Honey. Come on back." She turned and made her way to the back of the house. The front was pretty, but the back rivaled any professional job. She set the flat on a table and pulled off her gloves. "Would y'all like something to drink?"

"No thanks, we've just eaten." Honey answered for both of us.

Tabitha pulled out a chair. "Let's sit for a minute. I could use a rest." We sat around a white wrought-iron table.

Tabitha drank from a water bottle and screwed the lid back on. "I'm excited you're here to talk about working on a committee. I've been meaning to get more involved at the club, but I've had my hands full this summer with landscaping. We moved in this spring and the yard was a disaster. I imagined what it could look like and went to work."

"I didn't know you liked to garden. This looks like a professional job," Honey said.

"Thanks. My parents owned a landscaping business and I grew up helping them during the summers. I guess you could say I was blessed with a green thumb."

"It's evident in your work." I cleared my throat, "Do you have to use a lot of pesticides to keep such a beautiful yard?"

"Why are you really here, Skye? To talk about the committee or about pesticides?" She reacted to our shocked expressions. "That's right.

Penny called and told me all about how you practically accused her of Joan's murder. When she told me you were coming to interrogate me I said "Oh, no. Skye wouldn't do that. She wants me to work with her. But now I'm not so sure what you want."

Shame wrapped its spiny tendrils around my heart. "I do want you to work on the Fall Festival Committee. But the truth is we have to find out who killed Joan. Ginger, Honey's cousin, is being looked at as a possible suspect. Ginger wasn't involved and the jury's still out on Daniel. But if he didn't do it, we'll try and clear his name, too."

Her eyes glistened, threatening to spill tears any second. "I don't want to work on your committee and I don't have anything to say about Joan's murder. You're wasting your time. It's obvious Daniel did it. He's wanted Joan out of the way for years. That's all I'm saying. Find your own way back to your car." She turned and retreated into the safety of her house.

We got up to go. "Oh, boy. I think I hurt her feelings and I feel awful for deceiving her. I let desperation cloud my judgment."

"Don't feel too bad, Skye." Honey gave me a shoulder hug as we let ourselves out the gate. "She has easy access to organophosphates and she admitted knowing a lot about landscaping. What she didn't tell you is she's a nurse, giving her ready access to syringes as well."

I perked up. "That's right, Honey. I'd forgotten she's a nurse at Emory. That combination keeps her on the list. What's her motive, though?"

"I don't know. Jealousy?" Honey hopped in the driver's side while I settled in the passenger seat.

I looked at my watch. "It's only two o'clock. Why don't we head over to the library and see if we can dig up some dirt on the McGuire's?"

"Dig up dirt? Really, Skye."

We chuckled at my reference to digging up dirt, but my phone interrupted our reprieve from the gravity of our situation.

CHAPTER THIRTY-EIGHT

"Hi, hon. How are you?" Mitch's voice was a salve to my spirits.

"Hey! I'm good. Honey and I are on our way to the library to research the McGuires. They built the house on Candler."

"Where's Mother?"

I hadn't thought of Miss Charlotte all morning. Out of sight, out of mind. "Ginger offered to stay with her while we worked." I'd failed to consider what Mitch might think.

"Skye, I like Ginger, but do you think she's up to taking care of Mother? You said yourself, they didn't gee haw."

"Yeah, but that's not the case now. They get along pretty good." I motioned to Honey that I'd be off in a minute.

"I hope you're right. Mother's experienced a lot of trauma recently. I don't want to add to it." He really meant he didn't want me adding to her trauma.

I assured him I'd call Ginger and check on Miss Charlotte and go right home if I needed to.

When I called home, Ginger confirmed all was well. Miss Charlotte had gone back to bed and slept until lunch. They'd had tuna sandwiches, and had even taken Buddy outside to play for a while. Now she was relaxing in the recliner and Ginger told me to take all the time we needed.

"I decided to borrow your computer. I hope you don't mind. I'm researching soap recipes for my new venture!"

I told Honey about Ginger's own research as we whisked into the library parking lot about two-thirty. The librarian at the front desk directed us to the Georgia Room where Janice was shelving books. Happy to take a break, she showed us how to find old newspaper articles and excused herself to help another patron.

After a few minutes of reading, I sat back to rest my eyes. "There are lots of articles on Frederick and Martha McGuire. Seems they were quite the socialites in their time."

"Yeah, here's the obituary for Frederick," Honey said.

"Seems he died of natural causes in 1920. I haven't found one for Martha yet." I'd discovered Frederick McGuire, Jr., inherited the house and property in 1920 after his father died. I assumed his mother had died earlier.

"They obviously lived a busy life, but nothing suspicious jumps out at me," Honey said.

"Let's focus on Frederick, Jr. next. He inherited the property in 1920. Let's start there and move forward." We spent the next hour poring over articles hoping to find something about him. According to the lack of publicity he generated he must have lived a boring life compared to his parents.

"My eyes are crossing." Honey removed her reading glasses and rubbed her eyes. "Let's give up for today."

"I guess you're right. Let's hang it up." I stopped short of shutting off the machine when Frederick, Jr.'s name caught my eye. "Wait! I found his obituary."

"Make a copy and we'll read it later. I need to go the little girl's room." Honey headed out the door before I could say jack-rabbit. Janice ran a copy for me before I left to find Honey. She was in the lobby waiting on me.

"Let's go back to the house for a cup of coffee. I'm sure Ginger's ready for a break, and we can fill her in on the day's events." I planned to cook Mitch a hearty supper. Maybe with a full stomach, he'd forget I'd been gone all day.

I worried over nothing. Miss Charlotte dozed in the recliner and

Ginger had gone to sleep on the couch. Everything was quiet at the Southerland homestead.

Looking for attention, Buddy ran to me. I gave his neck a good scratch. He melted – rolled over and stuck his legs in the air. Thank God I hadn't received any calls yet, but it could be a matter of time. I was in love with the pooch.

"You've fallen for him haven't you?" Honey knew me like a book knows its cover. I nodded and rubbed Buddy's stomach until his leg moved like it was attached to a motor.

Ginger roused from her nap, sat up and stretched. "I thought I heard someone."

Not wanting to disturb Miss Charlotte, we moved our conversation into the kitchen.

I started the coffee while Honey retrieved the cups from the cabinet. I needed a little extra oomph so I doctored the coffee with mocha creamer and topped it off with mini marshmallows. The combination proved to be a big hit with the girls.

Ginger took a sip, "Ohh, this is good." She wrapped her hands around the cup. "Don't leave me hanging. What did y'all do today? Any more interviews?"

Honey and I started at the same time. "You go ahead," I said.

"No, you first." This conversation sounded much like the ones we had when we were deciding where to eat.

"We spoke to Tabitha Holbrook. She's the last partner on Joan's tennis team," I told her.

"And?" Ginger leaned in.

"Well . . ."

"She's a gardener," Honey interrupted. So much for letting me go first. "Her yard looked professionally landscaped and she did it herself. She didn't admit to using pesticides, but there's no way a yard can look that good without some kind of pest control."

"That don't exactly make her a killer, Honey. What's her motive?" Ginger poured herself another cup of coffee.

I took back the reins, "That's just it. We don't have one."
"Yeah," Honey said, "but that doesn't mean there isn't one."
Ginger sat back, releasing a beleaguered sigh.

CHAPTER THIRTY-NINE

"I know it sounds terrible for me to hope another person's found guilty of Joan's murder, but I'm so afraid." Ginger laid her head in her hands.

Honey patted her on the back. "We understand, Gin, remember when Skye and I were suspects? We were scared, too."

"Yeah, and things turned out okay for us. Wait and see, the truth will come out," I said.

Ginger's smile didn't reach her eyes. "I sure hope so. I can't take much more."

"Don't give up hope, Ginger. We might not know Tabitha's motive, but we do know she loves gardening and she works as a nurse which gives her access to needles."

We were still talking about Tabitha when Miss Charlotte entered the kitchen. "Is supper ready yet dear?"

Obviously she felt better.

I looked at my watch, "It's not quite time. I can fix an early supper if you want me to, and we can reheat it when Mitch gets in." I said the wrong thing.

"Oh, my, no! Mitch likes his food freshly cooked."

I hated to burst her bubble, but Mitch had been eating reheated leftovers for years. It didn't seem to bother him as long as he had something to eat. He didn't keep a tight schedule and circumstances often came up at the store requiring him to stay late.

"I'll plan on having it ready about six. That's when Mitch tries to get home. Maybe he won't be detained at the store tonight." My gesture appeased her, so she returned to the living room and Mitch's recliner. I wracked my brain to conceive something suitable for Miss Charlotte to eat, but came up short. I'd think about it later.

"Look, Skye," Honey said, "why don't Gin and I go on and let you rest before you have to cook for Lottie. I volunteer at the Cancer Center tomorrow morning, but I'll be free after lunch. Are you available to get together then?"

"I'll be happy to stay with Miss Charlotte, again. Today was a breeze, she slept most of the time you were gone."

"I really appreciate your help, Ginger. It'll free me up to help Honey with the investigation."

I addressed Honey. "Since you're going to be busy in the morning, I might run to the library and do more research on the McGuires." I itched to get back on the case.

"Honey, why don't you drop me off at Skye's on your way to volunteer? That way she can get an early start," Ginger said.

"Sounds like a good idea." Honey grabbed her purse and went to tell Miss Charlotte good-bye, but we found her reclined in Mitch's chair snoring away. Honey smiled and gave me a hug. "See ya' tomorrow, sugar."

After Honey and Ginger left, I collapsed in my favorite rocker and dozed off as soon as I relaxed.

A slight shake on my shoulder startled me. "Hi, babe, I'm home." My eyes flew open as I realized Mitch was home and I hadn't even started supper.

"What time is it?"

He looked at his watch, "Six-fifteen."

"I'm sorry, Mitch. I fully intended to have supper on the table at six, but I went right to sleep as soon as I sat down." Mitch was used to having an evening meal when he worked late. But I feared Miss Charlotte would hold me to the six o'clock time I'd promised her.

Speaking of Miss Charlotte, she woke up shortly after Mitch arrived.

I'm sure she possessed special radar that honed in on Mitch's voice alerting her to wake up.

I finally placed cheese-toast sandwiches and soup on the table around seven.

After supper, Mitch and Miss Charlotte retreated to the living room while I cleaned the kitchen. When I finished, I found Mitch in his recliner and Miss Charlotte sitting in my favorite chair.

She watched Wheel of Fortune with rapt attention. "Over the Rainbow," she yelled. "My goodness, a child could have figured that one out." She noticed me standing in the room and retreated into her shell. "Oh, Skye, I didn't see you standing there."

Obviously. I had a hunch if Miss Charlotte let down her façade she wouldn't be much different from the rest of us. I longed to chip away at her crusty outside and discover the real Miss Charlotte. But the carefree person I'd observed withdrew inside as if she were afraid for anyone to see she had feelings.

I returned to my room so Miss Charlotte could have some time alone with Mitch. After I took a long bubble bath and settled in bed, I read the obituary I'd found on Frederick McGuire, Jr.

Frederick, Jr. and his wife Gloria had two surviving children, Samantha and Martin. *Martin?* Was he the present owner of the house? If so, the McGuires had passed down the historic house through generations.

When Mitch came to bed, I showed him the obituaries and explained how I believed Martin inherited the house his grandfather had built.

"Now we're getting somewhere. This information gives us a trail to follow. I can't wait to go to the library tomorrow." I placed the articles on the bedside table and turned off the lamp. I snuggled close to Mitch savoring the warmth from his body.

"Babe, please be careful. Just because this appears to be an old murder, doesn't mean the killer isn't walking around somewhere and doesn't want to be discovered."

CHAPTER FORTY

inger arrived at nine. We'd already eaten breakfast, so I poured her a cup of coffee and offered her a doughnut. I gave her Miss Charlotte's medicine schedule and headed out the door with my information in hand.

The Georgia Room at the library was nearly empty. A couple of people sat at tables with their heads bent low studying their research. I headed straight to Janice's desk.

"Hi, Janice. Remember the McGuire family my friend and I researched?"

She peered at me over her half-glasses. "Sure do, and I'm so glad you came back. After you left, I remembered an article I'd seen recently while going through some papers. The name McGuire caught my attention. According to the article, Becky McGuire, of the same address as your house on Candler, went missing a couple of years ago."

"Are you serious?" I spoke louder than I intended.

"Sure am." She headed for a bank of cabinets and I followed so closely, I ran into her when she stopped. "I'm sorry. I'm anxious to read about her disappearance."

After several minutes of searching, she handed me the article. "Here it is. I'm going to leave it with you while I finish working on shelving books. Let me know if you need anything, I'll be glad to help."

For the next couple of hours, I devoured every article I found on

Martin and Becky McGuire. I discovered more than I ever dreamed. I sat back and closed my eyes to slow the whirlwind of information swirling in my mind.

Deep in thought, I literally jumped off the chair when someone shook me. "Honey, you took ten years off my life. I almost had a heart attack."

"Yeah, but you didn't. So all is well." She offered me a smile, hooked her purse on the back of a chair and took a seat. "Well, did you find anything?"

"Boy, did I. Take a look at these articles.""

She gasped as I handed her the most informative one on Becky's disappearance.

"What is it? You look like you've seen a ghost."

"I think I might have." She pointed to the picture of Martin. "Remember, I told Gabby his picture looked familiar?"

"Yeah."

"I know why now. I've seen him before. Remember when I rented a car while mine was in the shop? When I returned it there was a man already in the lobby."

"Was it Martin?"

"Yes. I remembered him because he was pacing back and forth and muttering to himself. When the agent returned, Martin practically yelled at him to hurry. I don't think I've ever seen anyone fly off the handle like that in public."

"What happened then?"

"He handed him the paperwork and Martin stormed out." She shook her head. "I have to admit I was shaken. I started to call Robert, but when he left, I didn't bother."

I pointed to the information she held. "Go ahead and finish reading about Becky's disappearance. This is all beginning to add up, now." She skimmed the first few sentences.

"Did you notice where he worked? Isn't that the name of the lab where Daniel works?" I couldn't wait for her to finish.

She looked where I pointed. "I believe you're right. I didn't see the connection. We'll have to ask Daniel if he knows him."

Honey checked the room, leaned in and spoke in a hushed whisper. "Wow, this is unbelievable." She pointed to the article. "Martin claimed Becky ran off with a lover and he never heard from her again. No wonder she was in the wall."

"My thoughts exactly. The police considered him a person of interest, but didn't have enough evidence to hold him. They didn't even have a body." I scooted closer to Honey, "There has to be a connection between the body and Martin. His tantrum at the car rental proves he has a volatile temper. Do you think Detective Haynes has put two and two together?"

"Well, if they haven't yet, they will. They're probably waiting on DNA results to verify the body belongs to Becky."

"Come on, Honey. Let's gather this information and take it to Detective Haynes. He won't be pleased we've stuck our noses into another investigation, but he needs to know about the incident at the agency. It's too important not to share."

Officer Donna pecked away at the computer in the police precinct. The only other person in sight was a guy with a cap pulled over his eyes and head laid back against the wall – probably sleeping. Officer Donna looked up and said, "May I help you?" before she noticed who we were. "Oh, you again. What did you do, find another body?"

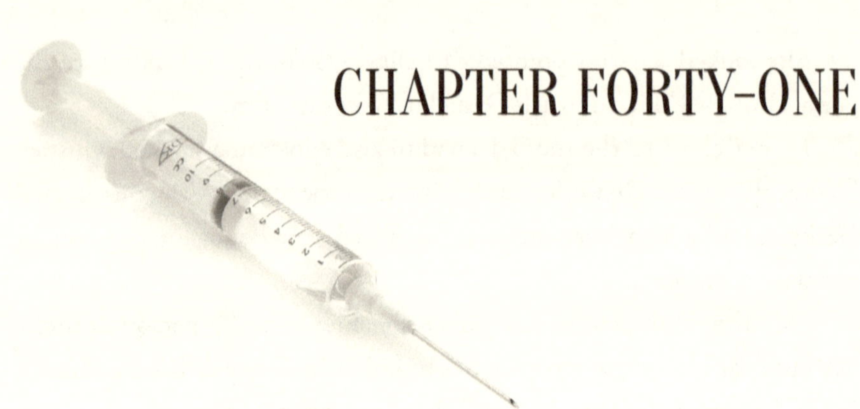

CHAPTER FORTY-ONE

She was the only one who found that funny.

"We're here to see Detective Haynes," Honey said with eyes of steel directed at Donna.

The laughter stopped and Donna sat up a little straighter. "Well, all righty then. Take a seat and I'll let him know you're here. It might be a while; he has someone in the office right now."

We made our way to the familiar seats. "I left the information about Martin and Becky in the car," I said.

Honey flashed a manila envelope. "I've got it."

"Good. I thought of something on the way over. If you saw Martin McGuire at the car rental, he couldn't have been out of the country."

"You're right. So he did lie. He must have been covering something up." Honey pulled out her mirror and lipstick. You'd think she was getting ready to see Robert instead of Detective Haynes. This reminded me I needed to make a stop by Merle Norman soon.

"I think the detective will be glad to get this information. Maybe he'll give us a little slack when he finds out we're trying to prove Daniel innocent of Joan's murder."

"I don't know. He didn't seem too impressed we'd helped solve Sylvia Landmark's case."

"That's true. We should share what we've learned about Martin McGuire and not mention we've been interviewing suspects in Joan's case. Let's go over all the information we've gathered when we get back to my place and decide if we have enough to share."

"Lordy, Skye. How did we get mixed up in a murder case involving a skeleton? If we help solve these cases they'll have to give us our own badges."

Detective Haynes appeared from his office ushering a disheveled woman down the short hall. Her wrinkled face revealed a life time of hard living. I imagined the detective saw the worst of humanity. At that moment, I respected his ability to bear the burdens he carried on those broad shoulders.

"Ladies, right this way." He stepped aside letting us go first.

We spent the next forty-five minutes discussing the information we'd unearthed as well as sharing the incident at the car rental store. He threw us a small crumb in return – they'd sent the skeleton's DNA for testing. He thanked us, but launched into a diatribe about staying out of police business. When he finished, he showed us to the door. I was more than ready to go home.

Honey called Ginger to see if she wanted a hamburger. None of us had eaten lunch, so I volunteered to go through the drive-through and pick up some fast-food. I ordered Miss Charlotte a salad in case she hadn't eaten.

We chowed down in the kitchen while Miss Charlotte napped in Mitch's recliner. Between bites, Honey told Ginger the story of Martin and Becky McGuire.

"I'm afraid y'all will forget my case now that you've gotten involved with the headless skeleton," she said.

Honey patted her hand. "Sugar, we wouldn't leave you hanging."

Great choice of words Honey. "Let's make a list and go over the suspects we've already interviewed."

"Great idea, Skye."

I grabbed pen and paper from a drawer and shoved it toward Honey. "Why don't you write down the names?"

"Okay, shoot."

"I'd put Mike Martin at the top of the list. He had motive and he just plain gave me the creeps," Ginger noted.

Honey wrote with a flourish. "There ya' go Gin. And I agree he had motive. He lost a much needed job because of Joan. People kill for much less."

"We interviewed Penny next," I said. "She definitely didn't like Joan, but was that motive enough to kill her?"

Honey wielded the pen pointing it at me like a weapon. "I think she withheld information. Maybe Joan was blackmailing her or something. I wouldn't put it past her." She jotted down Penny's name.

"That's conjecture," I stated.

"Yeah, but don't forget she's president of the garden club. She had ready access to organophosphates."

"That's right, but everybody we interviewed had access to the poison. That kind of throws a monkey wrench into the investigation."

Elbows on table, Gin laid her head in her hands. "How are we ever going to figure this out?" A tear rolled down Ginger's cheek.

I got up and gave her a hug. "Oh, honey, we'll figure it out." I wasn't sure how we'd do it, but I knew without a doubt Ginger was innocent. I cringed when I thought how judgmental I'd been when we first met. I'm so thankful my eyes were opened. Because of my willingness to accept Ginger where she was in her journey, I'd been the recipient of a fabulous friendship.

Honey reached in her purse, pulled out some Kleenex, and handed them to Ginger. "That's right. We won't stop until we prove your innocence." She steered the subject back to the suspects. "All right, who's next?"

Between sniffles, Ginger brought up the next person we interviewed. "Y'all went to talk to Mindy Tolbert at the Botanical Gardens while I stayed with Miss Charlotte. Right?"

"That's right." Honey looked my way. "I don't think Skye was too happy to be going back to the gardens after what happened last time we went." Honey laughed and Ginger joined in. "I can't help it, Skye.

You should have seen yourself come up out of that water like a jack-in-the-box."

"I'm sure it was hilarious." If Ginger felt better at my expense, so be it. I offered them a token smile.

"Why don't we move right along? Mindy had a strong motive. Daniel told her he wanted to work on his relationship with Joan. It was obvious she was in love with him and she could have killed Joan to get her out of the way."

"Yeah, and being the chief person over the vegetable gardens gave her ready access to all kinds of poisons."

"Her motive might be stronger than Mike's," Ginger said. "Who was the other person y'all talked to the same day?"

We simultaneously said, "Tabitha."

"I don't think she had much of a motive to kill Joan. I don't even know if we need to put her on the list of suspects," I said.

Honey ignored me and scribbled her name down anyway. "We might not have discovered a motive yet, but don't forget she's a landscape artist and knows how to use a syringe. I say we leave her on for now."

"Okay, but let's move Mindy to the top of the list. There's nothing like the revenge of a scorned woman. A show of hands please." Both girls raised their hands.

I jumped when the phone rang.

CHAPTER FORTY-TWO

I rarely received calls on the landline anymore. "Hello."

"Is this Ms. Southerland?" The unfamiliar male voice was pleasant enough.

"Yes. Can I help you?"

"I'm Steve. I work with Gabriela Miller. She's tied up with a client so she asked me to call and see if you could meet her at the McGuire house at five this afternoon."

"I'm not sure if we can meet there. The police deemed it a crime scene," I said. Honey and Ginger hung on to every word.

"Oh, she said to tell you she called and okayed it with a Detective Haynes."

An odd sensation gnawed at the pit of my stomach, but he said Gabby had gotten permission.

"Hold on a minute." I placed my hand over the receiver and asked Honey if she had any plans around five. Her eyebrows shot up, but she shook her head no.

"All right, tell Gabby we'll be there."

"Good. I'll confirm the five o'clock appointment with her." Steve sounded pleased he'd accomplished his task.

I hung up and explained to the girls what had transpired. "Wonder what she wants?"

I turned to Ginger. "I think that it might be better if I hired someone for a few days until Charlotte feels better. That pain medicine's thrown her for a loop and I don't want to take up your time."

"Don't worry about it, Skye. I told you it's no problem. I've gathered a lot of ideas for new scents for my soaps. And I feel like I'm giving something in return for all the help you've given me," Ginger said. "Besides, she reminds me of my grandma and she's given me some ideas for aromas I can try."

"All right, but if she's not better in a couple days I'll hire a sitter. I might even be able to get her assistant, Jennifer, to come help out."

With that settled, Honey and I left a little early. I wanted to swing by the shop and make sure I had everything I needed. This job was a big break for us.

"Honey, I just thought of something."

"Did it hurt?" Honey slapped her leg and laughed at her own little joke.

"Very funny, Einstein. Seriously, what if the police arrest Martin for Becky's murder? Then getting the job is a moot point."

"As Aunt Helen used to say, 'We'll cross that bridge when we get there. The house will still need to be repaired, the ruined furniture restored."

Lost in our thoughts the rest of the trip was quiet. A rare moment with Honey along.

Gabby's car wasn't in the driveway. Maybe the meeting with her client ran over. I knew how easy that could happen. "Come on, let's go in and wait on her." She'd given me a key so I could come by and take measurements if needed.

"It's dark in here with the curtains closed." I flipped the light switch, but only a small lamp responded. "Not much, but it'll help."

We passed the empty hole where Miss Charlotte found the skeleton. "That gives me the creeps. Who'd want to bury their dead wife in the wall? I bet it smelled worse than a skunk-sprayed dog. And I've smelled more than my share growing up in the mountains," Honey said.

"Add a little lime, and it's not so bad." The disembodied voice came from the shadows. A male figure stepped into the light.

With a squeaky voice I asked, "Martin McGuire?"

"The one and only."

"Skye, watch out, he's got a gun," Honey said.

"That's right, ladies, and you'd better do what I say."

Oh, dear Lord, please help us. Why didn't I listen when my gut feeling told me something wasn't right? You'd think I'd learn after a while, but I kept right on ignoring God's warning.

"So y'all think you've got this all figured out." He spoke to Honey, "That was a bad decision to run and tell the detective you saw me at the car rental. Playing with fire can get you in a lot of trouble."

Honey and I looked at each other.

"You're wondering how I know about that," Martin said. "Loose lips sink ships. I was at the police station when y'all decided to discuss Becky's disappearance. Lucky for me we happened to be there at the same time."

The guy in the ball cap who looked like he was sleeping!

"Why did you kill her?" If I kept him talking I could buy some time to think of an escape.

"Better yet why did you hide her in the wall?" Honey demanded.

"Why not put her in the wall? By the time I reported her missing, the decomp process had finished. They scoured this house with a fine tooth comb, but didn't find one shred of evidence. Who'd ever think to look in the walls of the house? It would have been the perfect murder if the tree hadn't fallen on the roof leaving the rain to weaken the walls."

Come on Skye, keep him talking. "I don't understand why you killed your wife. You owned the house and inherited your family's estate. How would Becky's death benefit you?"

"That's right. When I married Becky she had nothing. Her family lived on the other side of the tracks, if you know what I mean." He paused for a second. "It didn't matter, I loved her anyway."

"Then why kill her?"

"I didn't want to. She made me do it."

How many people have murdered and blamed the victim? With Martin's temper had he abused Becky?

"Oh, I see."

"No you don't see. She told me she was leaving to start a new life. She accused me of being abusive and wanted a divorce. She threatened to get at least half of everything. I couldn't let her get away with that. I worked hard for my money and I wasn't going to let her rob me blind."

He failed to mention he'd probably inherited most of his fortune.

Honey encouraged him to continue. "So that's why you killed her?"

His eyes glazed and his face tightened. "That's only part of the reason. I knew she was having an affair with someone. She denied it, but she couldn't fool me. She was a tricky one. I never could catch her. It didn't matter, I knew the real reason she was leaving. I wasn't going to let that harlot spend my money on another man. Like I said, she made me kill her."

"You killed her for having an affair you weren't even sure of?" Honey questioned him.

I heard a gasp and realized it was mine. We needed to keep him talking, but not at the expense of making him mad.

He snorted. "Well, I was ninety-nine percent sure. That was plenty for me. But it wasn't long until I discovered who she'd been seeing. I was looking through an old trunk in the attic when I found her diary. She was having an affair with one of my co-workers." He spit out the next words like they were venom, "Daniel Smith."

This time the gasp came from Honey. "Dr. Daniel Smith?"

"That's right. I had to go to work every day knowing he and Becky had been meeting behind my back. Can you imagine how humiliating that was?"

I nodded, hoping he'd continue. Then it dawned on me he was spilling his guts because he planned on killing us. I had to come up with a plan.

"That was bad enough, but when they passed me over at work and gave Daniel the administration position that should have been mine, that was the last straw. I was so angry I couldn't get along with anyone and eventually, they fired me. I determined I'd make Daniel pay."

"Oh, my goodness! You killed Joan!"

CHAPTER FORTY-THREE

"**B**rilliant deduction, Watson. Don't you think my plan worked perfectly? With his reputation as a playboy and the delivery method of the poison, I knew he'd be the main suspect."

"But Joan was innocent. She didn't do anything to you," I said.

Honey kept tilting her head to one side. When had she developed a nervous tick?

"Most unfortunate, but Daniel's to blame for her murder. He should have thought about the consequences of his actions."

Now Honey's eyes moved in the same direction. Why was she looking at my shoulder bag? Wait a minute, the Taser. I returned a slight nod of acknowledgement. I placed my hand on top of my bag waiting for the right opportunity.

While Martin continued talking I noticed Honey's hand go for a book on a small table. I prepared to grab the Taser. We only had one chance to make this work.

Honey threw the book at Martin hitting the gun, causing Martin to fire it. The sting in my left arm didn't hinder me from grabbing the Taser on the first try and shooting it at a startled Martin.

He fell to the ground convulsing as if he'd had a seizure. I glanced over only to find Honey shaking as if I'd shot her, too.

"Honey, snap out of it!"

"What do we do now?" The calm and rational Honey from a few minutes ago was now on the verge of a meltdown.

"I don't know. Call 911. Call Robert. Call somebody!" When I heard the sirens I couldn't help but say a little prayer of thanksgiving. *"Thank you, Jesus."*

The door burst open. Detective Haynes, gun pulled, was followed by a sea of cops decked out in S.W.A.T. gear. The detective's eyes went wide when he saw Martin writhing on the floor.

Detective Haynes holstered his gun and told the officers to stand down. He handcuffed Martin. "Well, ladies, a job well done." He looked at my arm. "You're bleeding, Ms. Southerland."

Sure enough, blood dripped from a gash in my arm. The bullet had grazed me when the gun went off. With my heightened adrenaline I hadn't felt the full effect of the wound. Now that I'd seen my open skin, the pain set in.

The detective pulled out his handkerchief, "Don't worry this is clean." He wrapped it around my wound. "That looks like it's going to take some stitches. You'll need to head to the hospital then come to the station and give us a statement later."

I heard a familiar voice ask, "Can we come in, now?" Ginger's head appeared inside the door.

"Yes. The scene's been neutralized." He turned to one of the officers and handed over Martin, "John, get him out of here."

Ginger hesitantly rounded the door. Leaning on her arm for support was Miss Charlotte.

"Ms. Southerland, Ms. Truelove, you can thank this little lady," he placed his hand on her shoulder, "for notifying us of your whereabouts."

"Ginger, how'd you know we were in trouble?"

"Gabby called after you'd left and I told her you were waiting on her at the house. She said she didn't have anyone call about a meeting. Right away, I got worried and called Detective Haynes."

"Come on, ladies, a group hug," Honey said. We all hugged, and Miss Charlotte did something I'll never forget. Standing beside me she looked at me with glistening eyes, "Oh, Skye, I was so worried." My heart melted. Maybe this was the breakthrough I'd been longing for.

Ginger took Miss Charlotte home and I called Mitch to tell him what happened. He said he'd meet me at the hospital. The Taser he'd bought for my safety had saved our lives.

It wasn't the stitches that hurt, but the needles they stuck into my gaping arm to numb my skin in preparation for the stitches. They wrapped my wound with gauze and told me go to my family doctor in ten days to have the stitches removed. I'd have a scar, left by the battle injury, reminding me how close I'd come to losing my life.

Mitch asked us if we wanted to eat before going to the police station. Neither one of us had an appetite. I wanted to get the interview over with and return to the comfort of my home.

Thank goodness Officer Donna wasn't on duty. I didn't think I could face her after the day I'd been through. Fortunately, we didn't have to wait, Detective Haynes came right out.

The next two hours Honey and I relayed the whole scene several times. We told him how Martin had called and pretended to work for Gabby and lured us to the house. We recounted the confession over and over for him. He questioned me, then Honey, then both of us, making sure our stories correlated.

I was surprised when the detective told us Martin had been a suspect in Joan's case as well as his wife's. They couldn't place him at the scene until Honey told him about Martin being at the car rental. They were able to find the car he'd rented and discovered the company had installed trackers on each car for insurance purposes. It recorded every stop Martin made as well as the day and time. They placed him at Joan's at the time of the murder. The DNA results from the skeleton had not come back from the lab yet, but they had his confession and the police had new evidence. Detective Haynes assured us Martin would never be a free man again.

The detective planned on calling Daniel to tell him the news and he exonerated Ginger from any wrong-doing. He thanked us for our help, but lectured us on how dangerous it could be to become involved in a murder investigation. He didn't have to tell me twice.

Christmas was around the corner. I couldn't believe how time had flown since Honey and I almost became statistics. Miss Charlotte went home on schedule with Jennifer helping her. Mitch and I talked about Miss Charlotte moving in with us. The family home needed more repairs than it was worth, and Miss Charlotte wasn't getting any younger. Mitch thought it would be a good idea to keep an eye on his mother's *medicinal* intake. I had mixed feelings, but I'd do whatever was best for Miss Charlotte.

Ginger couldn't thank Honey and I enough for our help. Her rehabilitation is going great and now that her life has settled down she's back to making her homemade products using the recipes she found online while Charlotte-sitting. She's even sold some on-line.

Honey and Robert are a hot item. They're together whenever they get the chance and Honey's hoping for an engagement ring for Christmas. I don't believe I've ever seen her so happy.

Nobody answered the ad for Buddy, so he's become a sweet part of our little family.

As for Mitch and I, we've grown closer than ever. Realizing how close I came to meeting death has caused us to appreciate the time we have with each other. Oh, and I finally got by Merle Norman and picked up some Romance Red lipstick. Mitch said I reminded him of a beautiful red rose when I wore it.